John Stuart Blackie

A Song of Heroes

John Stuart Blackie

A Song of Heroes

ISBN/EAN: 9783337181345

Printed in Europe, USA, Canada, Australia, Japan

Cover: Foto ©Andreas Hilbeck / pixelio.de

More available books at **www.hansebooks.com**

A SONG OF HEROES

A

SONG OF HEROES

BY

JOHN STUART BLACKIE

EMERITUS PROFESSOR OF GREEK IN THE UNIVERSITY OF
EDINBURGH; AUTHOR OF 'LAYS AND LEGENDS
OF ANCIENT GREECE,' ETC.

TO

ROBERT BROWNING,

POET, PHILOSOPHER, AND SCHOLAR,

THIS VOLUME

IS, WITH SINCERE ESTEEM AND BROTHERLY REGARDS,

𝕯𝖊𝖉𝖎𝖈𝖆𝖙𝖊𝖉

BY THE AUTHOR.

PREFACE.

PREFACES are in the general case to be avoided;
but there is something in the plan of this book,
that may be the better of a word of explanation.
I cannot say that it originally started with a conscious plan; but, once started, a plan with a native
instinct grew out of it; and the plan is this. It
selects a sequence of the most notable names in
European and West Asian history during a period
of more than three thousand years, and gives a
sketch of their lives, as the bearers and expon-
ents of the significant ages to which they belong.
These ages, as they strike the historical eye, are the
following: the patriarchal age, the age of Moses

and the Jewish law, the Hebrew monarchy, the age of Greek philosophy under Socrates and Plato, and of the Hellenisation of the East by Alexander the Great; then the Romanising of the West under Julius Cæsar, and the Christianising of both East and West by the preaching of the Apostles. As the natural sequence of this comes the Christianisation of the extreme West of Europe, by the Celtic Churches, with their headquarters in Galloway, Ireland, and Iona; and in the secular world, the birth of new monarchies in Europe to take the place of the disrupted Roman Empire. In the spiritual world the sacerdotal aristocracy of Rome forms of course a prominent feature, introducing, by the great law of reaction, the religious reformation of the sixteenth century. The assertion of the rights of free Individualism in the Church was naturally followed by a similar protest against absolute power in the head of the State: this brings us to the age of the great civil war in England, and the action of popular Parliaments in the government of modern European States. The

century following saw two new scenes in the grand
drama of social progress : the creation of a great
democratic Republic beyond the Atlantic, and the
repression of a despotic centralisation in Europe,
by the long series of wars that sprang out of the
violence of the French Revolution. In selecting
the persons to be the bearers of these significant
moments of social progress, I was guided, as the
reader will readily see, by three considerations: first,
I had to look for a real hero, which means not
only a strong man and a mighty force, but a great
man—that is, a man great in all that most distin-
guishes man from the lower animals, and exhibits
most of his kinship to the Creator ; a man morally
great, the champion of a noble cause, and inspired
in all his actions by that love which St Paul stamps
as the fulfilling of the law. In the next place, I
had to choose a character which should be not
only noble in its moving power, but picturesque
and dramatic, as far as possible, in its situations
and incidents ; and again, I had to consider the
place where I stood, and the people whom I ad-

dress, whose sympathies I could not hope to enlist in favour of characters, however noble, who were not part of their natural inheritance, and of their living environment. Of these considerations the first will explain why I have introduced Napoleon, only as a background to the French wars which brought him into prominence; as also why the Popes in the middle ages serve only the same subsidiary purpose, in connection with Martin Luther. Good men and great men they might be individually; but being spokesmen and standard-bearers of a cause essentially selfish, sacerdotal, and unheroic, as a singer of pure human heroes I could have nothing to do with them. The two other considerations will explain why I have chosen Alfred rather than Charlemagne, as the representative of modern European monarchies; and, had I been a German writing for Germans, I should certainly have planted Barbarossa or some of the Hohenstauffen in the niche which, as a Scot, I was proud to assign to Wallace and Bruce; while for similar patriotic reasons, the place of honour in

the more recent history of Britain has been as-
signed to Cromwell, which in a German atmo-
sphere would have fallen to Gustavus Adolphus, or
the great Prussian Frederick. So much for the
historical significance of this little book ; in which,
if the poetical treatment should unhappily fall
under the censure of the judicious critic, the less
fastidious student of human fates may not fail to
find a fair amount of encouraging stimulus and
healthy nutriment. For the sake of such students
I shall be happy to have pleased less, that I may
instruct more.

EDINBURGH, 1st November 1889.

CONTENTS.

CANTO I.—THE OLD WORLD.

CANTO II.—THE MIDDLE AGES.

CANTO III.—THE NEW WORLD.

CANTO I.

THE OLD WORLD

ABRAHAM.

I WILL sing a song of heroes
   Crowned with manhood's diadem,
Men that lift us, when we love them,
   Into nobler life with them.

I will sing a song of heroes
   To their God-sent mission true,
From the ruin of the old times
   Grandly forth to shape the new ;

Men that, like a strong-winged zephyr,
   Come with freshness and with power,
Bracing fearful hearts to grapple
   With the problem of the hour ;

Men whose prophet-voice of warning
 Stirs the dull, and spurs the slow,
Till the big heart of a people
 Swells with hopeful overflow.

I will sing the son of Terah,
 ABRAHAM in tented state,
With his sheep and goats and asses,
 Bearing high behests from Fate;

Journeying from beyond Euphrates,
 Where cool Orfa's bubbling well
Lured the Greek, and lured the Roman,
 By its verdurous fringe to dwell;[1]

When he left the flaming idols,
 Sun by day and Moon by night,
To believe in something deeper
 Than the shows that brush the sight,

---

[1] Edessa, according to a very general Jewish tradition, was the Ur of the Chaldees; but some modern inquirers prefer Mugheir, on the right bank of the Euphrates, in the bitumen district, about 120 miles above the sea.

And, as a traveller wisely trusteth
 To a practised guide and true,
So he owned the Voice that called him
 From the faithless Heathen crew.

And he travelled from Damascus
 Southward where the torrent tide
Of the sons of Ammon mingles
 With the Jordan's swelling pride,

To the pleasant land of Shechem,
 To the flowered and fragrant ground
'Twixt Mount Ebal and Gerizim,
 Where the bubbling wells abound;

To the stony slopes of Bethel,
 And to Hebron's greening glade,
Where the grapes with weighty fruitage
 Droop beneath the leafy shade.

And he pitched his tent in Mamre,
 'Neath an oak-tree tall and broad,

And with pious care an altar
    Built there to the one true God.

And the voice of God came near him,
    And the angels of the Lord
'Neath the broad and leafy oak-tree
    Knew his hospitable board ;

And they hailed him with rare blessing
    For all peoples richly stored,
Father of the faithful, elect
    Friend of God, Almighty Lord.

And he sojourned 'mid the people
    With high heart and weighty arm,
Wise to rein their wandering worship,
    Strong to shield their homes from harm.

And fat Nile's proud Pharaohs owned him,
    As a strong God-favoured man,
Like Osiris, casting broadly
    Largess to the human clan.

And he lived long years a witness
 To the pure high-thoughted creed,
That in the ripeness of the ages
 Grew to serve our mortal need.

Not a priest, and not a churchman,
 From all proud pretension free,
Shepherd-chief and shepherd-warrior,
 Human-faced like you and me ;

Human-faced and human-hearted,
 To the pure religion true ;
Purer than the gay and sensuous
 Grecian, wider than the Jew.

Common sire, whom Jew and Christian,
 Turk and Arab, name with praise ;
Common as the sun that shines
 On East and West with brothered rays.

MOSES.

I will sing high-hearted Moses,
  By the Nile's sweet-watered stream;
In a land of strange taskmasters,
  Brooding o'er the patriot theme ;

Brooding o'er the bright-green valleys
  Of his dear-loved Hebrew home,
Whence the eager pinch of Famine
  Forced the Patriarch to roam ;

Brooding o'er his people's burdens,
  Lifting vengeful arm to smite

When he saw the harsh Egyptian
　Stint the Hebrew of his right ;

Brooding far in lonely places,
　Where on holy ground unshod,
He beheld the bush that burned
　With unconsuming flame from God.

Saw, and heard, and owned the mission,
　With his outstretched prophet-rod
To stir plagues upon the Pharaoh,
　Scorner of the most high God ;

God who brought His folk triumphant
　From the strange taskmaster free,
And merged the Memphians, horse and rider,
　In the deep throat of the sea.

Then uprose the song of triumph,
　Harp and timbrel, song and dance ;
And with firm set will the hero
　Led the perilous advance.

And he led them through the desert
     As a shepherd leads his flock,
Breaking spears with cursed Amalek,
     Striking water from the rock.

And he led them to Mount Sinai's
     High-embattled rock ; and there,
'Mid thick clouds of smoke and thunder
     That like trumpet clave the air,

To the topmost peak he mounted,
     And with reverent awe unshod,
As a man with men discourseth,
     So he there communed with God.

Not in wild ecstatic plunges,
     Not in visions of the night,
Not in flashes of quick fancy,
     Darkness sown with gleams of light,

But with calm untroubled survey,
     As a builder knows his plan,

Face to face he knew Jehovah
And His wondrous ways with man ;

Ways of gentleness and mercy,
Ways of vengeance strong to smite,
Ways of large unchartered giving,
Ever tending to the right.

In the presence of the Glory,
What no mortal sees he saw,
And from hand that no man touches
Brought the tables of the Law,

Law that bound them with observance,
Lest untutored wit might stray,
Each man where his private fancy
Led him in a wanton way,

Law that from the life redeemed them
Of loose Arabs wandering wild,
And to fruitful acres bound them
Where ancestral virtue toiled ;

Law that dowered the chosen people
With a creed divinely true,
Which subtle Greek and lordly Roman
Stooped to borrow from the Jew.

DAVID.

I WILL sing the son of Jesse,
    Whom the prophet's voice did call,
Not by haughty-hearted bearing,
    Lofty looks, and stature tall ;

But by eyes of arrowy brightness,
    And by locks of golden hue,
And by limbs of agile lightness,
    Fair and comely to the view ;

And by earnest, wise demeanour,
    And by heart that knew no fear,
And a quick-discerning spirit
    When a danger might be near.

Him from watching of the sheepfold,
   And from tending of the ewes,
To be ruler of the people,
   Samuel's prophet-eye did choose.

From the softly-swelling pasture,
   Grassy mead, and rocky scars;
From lone converse with the mild-faced
   Moon and silent-marching stars;

From the lion and the she-bear,
   When they leapt the wattled pen,
To a fight with worse than lions,
   Tiger-hearted, bloody men.

To the struggle for a kingdom,
   To confusion of his foes,
To the splendid cares of reigning,
   Him the God-sent prophet chose;

Chose, nor waited long. A kingship
   Reigned in bosom of the boy,

And his hand with kingly instinct
    Leapt to find a king's employ.

And he found it when the giant
    Philistine of haughty Gath,
With a boastful, proud defiance,
    Mailed in insolence, crossed his path.

Quailed the armies of the people,
    Quailed King Saul upon his throne,
Quailed the marshalled heads of battle ;
    Strength in DAVID lived alone.

And he took nor spear nor harness,
    But with calm composèd look,
In his hand he took a sling,
    And five smooth pebbles from the brook ;

And he prayed the God of battles,
    And in 'mid the host alone
Prostrate laid the boastful champion
    With a sling and with a stone.

Now his road was paved to greatness :
  On the right hand of the throne
High he sate ; but mighty monarchs
  Love to reign and rule alone.

Saul pursued the people's darling
  With keen hatred's heavy stress,
From rock to rock, from cave to cave,
  Of the houseless wilderness,

Like a hunted thing.   He wandered,
  From all bonds of fealty free,
Till the hour to honour DAVID
  Came in God's foreknown decree.

Judah claimed him ; Israel followed
  Judah's trumpet-note ; and all,
From Hermon's mount to well of Sheba,
  Streamed to royal DAVID's call.

And he stormed the hill of Zion,
  Where the rock-perched Jebusite

From his stiff ancestral fastness
  Vainly strove to prove his might.

And he smote the men of Moab,
  And the fierce Philistian crew,
And o'er the ruddy cliffs of Edom
  Passed, and proudly cast his shoe.

From Damascus' gardened beauty
  Home he brought the golden spoil,
And Phœnician Hiram sent him
  Greeting from his sea-girt isle.

And he brought the ark that shrined
  The God-hewn tables of the Law,
Safely on the rock of Zion
  To be kept with reverent awe;

Brought it with a pomp of people,
  With a sounding march of glee,
Harp and hymn, and shouts of holy
  Triumph, billowing like the sea!

Not in mail of forceful warrior,
   Not with spear, and not with sword,
With a linen ephod girded,
   Danced the king before the Lord ;

Danced with lusty beat, not recking,
   In the stoutness of his cheer,
How solemn fools and dainty maids
   Might curve their lofty lips and jeer.

What remained?—Jehovah honoured,
   From all foes a proud release,
What remained to top his fulness?
   DAVID now might die in peace.

Only one fair hope was stinted,
   To the God of DAVID's line
On the summit of Moriah
   High to pile a costly shrine !

Not all things to all are granted ;
   To his son, the wisest man,

DAVID left with templed state
To crown his life's high-reaching plan,

Then died.   No kinglier king was ever
Seated on a kingly seat,
Shepherd, soldier, minstrel, monarch,
In all sorts a man complete.

SOCRATES.

In the case of a name of such wide significance as Socrates, it were superfluous to encumber the page with any display of learned notes. Suffice it to say that everything in the ballad is strictly historical, and taken directly from the original authorities. The indifference shown by Socrates to the ἀνάγκαι or necessary laws of physical science, as contrasted with the freedom of practical reason in which moral science delights, is distinctly emphasised by Xenophon in the opening chapters of the 'Memorabilia'; and the argument with the atheist—a little perking, self-sufficing creature, as atheists are wont to be—will be found at full length in the same sensible and judicious writer. It is this argument, commonly called the argument from design, that, passing through the eloquent pages of Cicero in his book 'De Naturâ Deorum,' has formed the groundwork of all works on Natural Theology up to the present time ; and it is an argument that, however misapplied here and there by shallow thinkers and presumptuous dogmatists, has its roots so deep in the instincts of all healthy humanity, and in the very essence of reason, that, though it may be illustrated indefin-

itely by example, it never can have anything either added
to its certainty or abstracted from its significance. The
early occupation of Socrates as a moulder of statues is men-
tioned by Pausanias ; and the name of Critias is introduced
to indicate the offence given by the free-mouthed talk of the
great teacher to the leaders of the political parties of his
time, which may have had as much to do with his martyrdom
as the charge of irreligion that, according to Xenophon, was
the main count of the indictment against him. His big
round eye, and other features of his personal appearance,
are minutely and humorously described by the same author
in the 'Banquet.'

I WILL sing a Greek, the wisest

Of the land where wisdom grew

Native to the soil, and beauty

Wisely wedded to the true.

SOCRATES, the general sire

Of that best lore which teaches man

In a reasoned world with reason

Forth to shape his human plan.

Not of fire he spake, or water,

Sun or moon, or any star,

Wheeling their predestined courses,
From all human purpose far.

Booted not to ask what fuel
Feeds the Sun, or how much he
Than the lady Moon is bigger
When she sails up from the sea.

Fool is he whose lust of knowing
Plumbs the deep and metes the skies;
Only one great truth concerns thee,
What is nearest to thine eyes.

Know thyself and thine; cast from thee
Idle dream and barren guess;
This the text of thy wise preaching,
Reason's prophet, SOCRATES.

Him in school of honest labour
Nature reared with pious pains,
With no blood from boasted fathers
Flowing in his sober veins.

As a workman works, he stoutly
   Plied his task from day to day ;
For scant silver pennies moulding
   Tiny statues from the clay.

But, when thought was ripe, obedient
   To the God-sent voice within,
Forth he walked on lofty mission,
   Truth to preach and souls to win.

Not the lonely wisdom pleased him,
   Brooding o'er some nice conceit ;
But where the many-mingling strife
   Of man with man made quick the street,

There was he both taught and teacher ;
   In the market where for gain
Eager salesmen tempt the buyer ;
   By Athena's pillared fane ;

In the Pnyx, where wrangling faction
   Thunders from a brazen throat,

And the babbling Demos holds
  The scales that tremble on a vote;

In the pleasant Ceramicus,
  Where the dead most honoured sleep,
In Piræus, where the merchant
  Stores the plunder of the deep.

There was he with big round eye
  Looking blithely round; and ever
He was centre of the ring
  Where the talk was swift and clever.

There, like bees around a hive
  Buzzing in bright summer weather,
Flocked, to hear his glib discourse,
  Sophist, sage, and fool together.

Statesmen came, and politicians,
  Strong with suasive word to sway;
Alcibiades, bold and brilliant,
  Dashing, confident, and gay.

Critias came with tearless stoutness,

   Sharp to wield the despot's power;

Aristippus, wise to pluck

   The blossom from the fleeting hour.

Came a little man, an atheist,

   Said in gods he could believe

If with eyes he might behold them;

   What we see we must believe.

Said the son of Sophroniscus,

   " Do you see yourself, or me ?

You may see my hand, my fingers,

   But myself you cannot see.

" When I spread my guests a banquet,

   Delicate with dainty fish,

Though unseen, unnamed, unnoted,

   'Twas a cook that sauced the dish.

" In the tragic scene, when mountain,

   Rock, and river, well combined,

Hold the sense, the show delights thee,
  But the showman lurks behind.

"So in all the shifting wonder
  Of the star-bespangled pole,
What we see is but the outward
  Seeming of the unseen soul.

"Let not shows of sense confound thee,
  Nothing works from reason free;
All within, without, around thee,
  Holds a god that speaks to thee."

So he talked and so he reasoned,
  Casting seeds of truth abroad,
Seeds that grow with faithful tendance
  Up to central truth in God.

But not all might thole his teaching;
  Weak eyes shrink when light is nigh,
Many love the dear delusion
  That lends glory to a lie.

'Mid the throng of gaping listeners,
  Idle danglers in the street,
When from front of vain pretender
  Deft he plucked the crude conceit,

Many laughed; but with a sting
  Rankling sore in bitter breast,
One departed, and another,
  Like a bird with battered crest.

And they brewed strong hate together,
  And with many a factious wile
Drugged the people's ear with slander,
  Stirred their hearts with sacred bile.

And they gagged his free-mouthed preaching;
  At Religion's fretful call
He must answer for his teaching
  In the solemn judgment-hall.

And they hired a host of pleaders,
  Subtle-tongued like any thong,

To confound weak wits with phrases,
　To convert most right to wrong.

And they mewed him in a prison,
　And they doomed him there to die,
And he drank the deathful hemlock,
　And he died, as wise men die,

With smooth brow, serene, unclouded,
　With a bright, unweeping eye,
Marching with firm step to Hades,
　When the word came from on high.

ALEXANDER.

I WILL sing of ALEXANDER,
　Macedonia's peerless boy,
In whose veins the blood of heroes
　Ran like rivers in their joy.

In his father's camp at Pydna
　Up he grew in ruddy grace,
Lithe of limb and tight of sinew,
　And with eager forward face.

First to run the race with racers,
　First to mount the restive steed,
First to chase the stag fleet-footed
　O'er the hills with flying speed.

Nor in feats of muscle merely,
  But in tricks of wit excels,
Drinking wisdom at Stagira,
  From the master-thinker's wells.

Born a king, the charm of kingship
  Went with him; and where he came,
Subtle Greek and rude Triballi
  Owned the virtue of his name.

Petty strifes might not detain him;
  Great souls long for large expanse;
Europe's age-long feud with Asia
  Claimed the service of his lance.

And he passed the stream of Helle,
  Where the Sea-nymph's fervid boy
With a thousand-masted navy
  Crossed to curb the pride of Troy.

And his eager foot he planted
  On that ten years' battle-ground,

And flung his war-gear off, and gaily
  Round Pelides' grassy mound

Rode three times; and with his captains
  In devout self-dedication
Crowned his tomb with bloom of flowers,
  And poured sweet oil of consecration.

Thence with foot that knew no resting,
  And a soul that spurned delay,
On to thy steep banks, Granicus,
  Where in bristling close array

Stood Darius' high-trained legions
  In proud pomp of glittering mail,
And from bend of bows gigantic
  Pouring arrows thick as hail,

Vainly; never pride of Susa
  Blocked to free-souled Greece the road;
Through surging tide and slippery bank
  On the Macedonian strode,

And stood white-plumed a victor. Onward
   Where the Sardian gold was stored,
Where the knot of Fate, the Gordian,
   Gaped to greet the Grecian sword.

Onward by the steep sea-ladders
   Where Pamphylia's tideful wave
Timed its swell to leave free passage
   To the footsteps of the brave.

Onward where high-ridged Amanus
   Towered o'er Issus' widespread waters,
Where Damascus' leafy gardens
   Wove green bowers for Syria's daughters.

Onward where the hold of Hiram,
   Sea-girt Tyre, his might defied;
But with heart that never fainted,
   O'er its haughty-crested tide

He flung a highway. Tyre submissive
   Bowed her neck: stout Gaza yields,

And hoary-centuried Egypt welcomed
  To her broad sweet-watered fields,

With people's shout and priestly blessing,
  Macedonia's marvellous boy.
He, unresting, through the sandy
  Desert, with prophetic joy,

Marched to Libya's green Oasis,
  Where, with mystic word and sign,
Hornèd Ammon's priestly spokesman
  Stamped his mission for divine.

Memphis now shall bow to Hellas:
  In great ALEXANDER's soul
Rose, God-sent, a pregnant fancy,
  Where the Coptic waters roll,

By the lake of Mareotis,
  By old Pharos' rocky isle,
There to found a mighty city
  Where the Greek should rule the Nile,

And he marked it out with omens,
  Bravely streeted east and west,
With the name of Alexander
  Stamped upon its stony breast.

Mighty city, home of science,
  Nurse of Commerce, queen of trade,
Whence Greek wit and Christian saintship
  Rayed a glory largely shed ;

Where the reasoned faith of Plato,
  Calmly measuring forth the true,
Shook hands with the prophet-passion
  Of the fiery-hearted Jew,

Both divine. But ALEXANDER
  Marched, blind pioneer of God,
With Fate behind and Fate before him,
  Eastward on his conquering road ;

Eastward, where far-sung Euphrates
  Pours his fattening waters wide,

Where from snowy-capped Niphates
　　Tigris rolls her foamy tide

To the plain of Gaugamela,
　　Where, in long-drawn tented show,
All the pride of golden Persia
　　Stood expectant of the foe !

Firmly stood the Persian battle,
　　Making wise Pausanias quake ;
But in soul of ALEXANDER
　　Swelled a tide no bar could break.

Like a mighty unmoored trireme
　　Drifting helmless from the blast,
Great Darius with his princes
　　O'er the Zagrian mountains passed :

There to seek 'mid traitor-Bactrians
　　Refuge, which more wisely he,
From his generous-hearted victor,
　　Might have craved on bended knee

At Babylon or royal Susa,
    Where the gold is piled in bales,
And Choaspes laves the meadows
    Where the fruitful green prevails.

Or 'mid pomp of stately pillars,
    Where Persepolis nursed the dream
Of the haughty-hearted Xerxes,
    To lay bonds on Helle's stream.

Here the victor paused; but Pause
    Made short call on ALEXANDER.
As a foam-faced mountain-torrent,
    With a gentle slow meander

Flows a space, then, as impatient
    Of inglorious ease, his motion
Spurs, and with exultant billow
    Roars at thunder-speed to ocean,

So he took short holiday,
    From golden bowls the red wine drinking,

With song and dance and pastime gay,
　And every power that strangles thinking.

Then uprose, and mailed his breast,
　Helmed his head, and looked around,
Finely pricked with eager joyaunce,
　Like a keen unkennelled hound.

On to Oxus, to Jaxartes,
　Where great Cyrus set a bound
To the loose unchastened Scythians,
　Like a tempest drifting round.

Some drew back : but ALEXANDER
　Knew not back ; and as on wings,
Up the steep-faced Bactrian fastness
　Deftly climbs, and bravely brings

Fair Roxana, blooming daughter
　Of the king, to be his bride.
What remained ?　Paropamisus,
　With its mountain-rampart wide,

Signed him onwards.   He might never
  Rest, till he prevailed to bind
With strong bonds of human kinship
  Westmost Greece and Eastmost Ind.

Onward, onward !   O'er thy birdless
  Steep, Aornos, he prevailed,
Which the stout son of Alcmena
  Three times dared, and three times failed.

Him the fort of Dionysus,
  Nysa, praised by the Hindoo,
With its wreaths of cooling ivy,
  And its groves of laurel, knew.

On the banks of the Hydaspes
  Porus stood, high-statured king,
With his elephants and chariots
  Bristling wide from wing to wing.

Breast-high marched the Macedonian
  Through its flood, nor knew to cease

From the shock of spears, till Porus
  Bowed the subject knee to Greece.

Indus with its seven mouths hailed him,
  Tideful ocean owned his rule,
And with grateful grace to Neptune
  There he sacrificed a bull.

Westward then with work accomplished,
  Through a wide unwatered waste,
Through thy burning sands, Gedrosia,
  Back his stout-souled march he traced :

Back to Babylon. There the nations,
  In the garb of gladness dressed,
Sent their missioned chiefs to greet him
  Umpire of the East and West.

But the gods would have him. Grandly
  What he proudly sought he gained :
Greece had conquered the Barbarian ;
  Where he throned her, she remained.

CÆSAR.

I HAVE sung the Greek.   The Roman
    Now stands forth in iron mailed,
Who by patient plan, and manly
    Will, and might of hand prevailed;

Who, by clod-subduing labour,
    Rose, hard toil and sober cheer,
Stern-faced Law and strict obedience,
    Sacred reverence and fear;

Fell, by overgrowth of Fortune,
    Fell, by insolence of sway,
When in pride of strength the strong man
    Tramped the weak man in the clay;

Fell, by sacred greed of having,
  All the trash that gold can buy,
Piles of grandeur, seas of glitter,
  Shows that feed the lustful eye;

Acres, gardens, gladiators,
  Fish-ponds, towers that flaunt the sky,
Purple pomp and pillowed pleasure,
  And a wine-cup seldom dry,

All things; only not a common-
  Hearted zeal for common good,
With a fevered lust of getting,
  Each man what he nearest could—

Not as brother strives with brother,
  But with rage of tigerhood,
Plunging, tearing on to power
  Through seas of bribery and blood.

But not all were vile. Some wildly
  Fought and foamed like fretted cattle;

Some, with lofty ken far-viewed,
    And lofty aim controlled the battle.

Such was CÆSAR ; neither weakly
    Shrinking from a forceful blow,
Nor with insolent triumph trampling
    In the mire a fallen foe.

Bred to fearless, firm directness
    In the soldier's kingly school,
In an age when only swords
    Gave strength to stand or right to rule,

Step by step with measured boldness,
    Wise to wait the ripening hour,
Quick to seize the breeze of favour,
    Up the strong man clomb to power.

Fluent talkers in the forum
    Sway the passion of the hour ;
But when Fate will seal her charter,
    Then the soldier comes with power.

CÆSAR now is Consul : seated
  Bravely in his curule chair,
With his rods and with his lictors,
  What is CÆSAR scheming there?

He hath crushed the Spanish brigands ;
  With sharp sword and strong decree,
O'er the Lusitanian mountains
  Pushed the Empire to the sea.

Now he'll lot the land to tillers,
  Strangle violence with law,
Drag to public reprobation
  Grasping hand and greedy maw.

Laws for peace : but peaceful glory
  Might not slake great CÆSAR's thirst ;
Where an arm might strike for mastery,
  There he panted to be first.

Pompey, with his pictured toga,
  Lopped the pride of Mithridates,

Cleared the seas of roving robbers,
   Wedded Tiber to Euphrates;

What shall Cæsar do? His boyhood's
   Memory nursed the glorious day
When mighty Marius, seven times Consul,
   To the fierce Celts blocked the way,

Drifting Romeward like a deluge;
   He, like Marius, would go forth,
And with Roman sword and sentence
   Tame the rude hordes of the North.

Nevermore shall Teut or Cimber,
   Nursed in Hyperborean snows,
Pour their wasteful swarms, like locusts,
   Where fair-fielded Padus flows.

Gaul was vexed with fevered faction;
   German and Helvetian hordes,
Westward with wild fury ramping,
   Call for sweep of Roman swords.

At Bibracte CÆSAR smote them,
  And in fine short-sworded line,
Grappling as a Roman grapples,
  Drave the Teuts across the Rhine.

Hardy Belgæ, stout-thewed Nervii,
  Sober water-drinking men,
On the banks of Meuse and Sambre
  Bowed the neck to CÆSAR then.

Suevi, clad with coats of deer-skin,
  Match for the immortal gods,
Felt that more than gods were near them,
  Where great CÆSAR showed his rods.

Not the westmost sailor Bretons,
  Flowed about with briny tides,
Can maintain their rocky townships
  Where great CÆSAR's soul presides.

Utmost Britain, Gaul's last refuge,
  Now his foot of venture knows :

Where the sea-mews round the white cliffs
    Sweep, where Thames majestic flows,

Victor he stood, and with prophetic
    Glance the time not distant saw
When the rude and painted Nomads,
    In stern school of Roman law

Trained to manhood, would rejoice
    In the grace of fixed abodes,
Roman towns and Roman villas,
    Roman camps and Roman roads.

Ten years' toil have born such fruitage;
    From Britannia's cloudy home
To blue Rhone, all breathe with safety
    'Neath the sheltering wing of Rome.

What reward shall be to Cæsar,
    Who hath made his country great?
Shall he march in pomp of triumph,
    Crowned with laurel, through the gate?

Shall ten thousand throats salute him
  Consul twice with loud acclaim ;
Consul, Censor, every title
  That can top a Roman name ?

Ask the Senate. No ; no grateful
  Thanks come from patrician breast,
Faction-mongers, plotters, hirelings,
  In the robe of statesmen dressed.

Him they fear ; and 'fore his kingly
  Glance with conscious guilt they cower,
Who with unbribed hand will rudely
  Stint their merchandise of power.

Mighty men to fling bravadoes ;
  But when CÆSAR claimed his right
At the gates of Rome, great Pompey
  With his minions winged their flight

To the far Brundisian refuge ;
  Thence across the Adrian foam,

There to head the Asian muster
    'Gainst the noblest man in Rome.

Vainly ; not who doubts and wavers,
    Never sure and ever late,
But who strikes with swift directness
    Is the minister of Fate.

Not Pharsalia's plains shall save thee,
    Pompey, with thy craven crew ;
Prideful greed that grew to rashness,
    In God's time shall have its due.

Proud patricians, purple-vested
    Foplings in soft luxury born,
Them stout CÆSAR's hard-faced veterans
    Mowed like swathes of bending corn.

Whither now ? Not yet hath CÆSAR's
    Foot adventurous reached the Nile ;
There, from sacred seats, on Pompey
    Frowning Fate might learn to smile.

Pompey deemed : but fallen greatness
  In a friend oft finds a foe ;
On the shores of Nile the headless
  Pompey lies in ghastly show.

Mighty Pompey dead ; and Cato,
  With stiff neck and lofty head,
Holding guard in Honour's temple,
  Where the god within had fled.

Stoic Cato 'mid the ruins
  Of old Rome the Fate defied,
And proudly on the coast of Afric
  With self-planted dagger died.

Now the big round globe is CÆSAR's ;
  What thing now shall CÆSAR do,
Through those veins corrupt and fevered
  Healthy pulses to renew ?

He will be their needful master,
  By firm law and not by blood —

Consul, Cæsar, Imperator—
    Strangling faction in the bud.

Not the triumph of a party,
    But a firm-compacted State,
Where every limb subserves the headship,
    Shall make mighty Cæsar great.

Not with Sulla's butcher-vengeance,
    At his word red slaughter flows,
But with large and free forgiveness
    He repays the hate of foes.

Not from feeble-blooded lordlings,
    Hollow hearts in purple dressed,
But from men he made the Senate,
    Proved the bravest and the best.

He would prune the flaunting plumage
    Of the fine soft-feathered crew,

Borne about by slaves in litters,
    Lest the mud should soil their shoe.

But he strove in vain : the outward
    Reverent show he might compel,
But their hearts with deadly rancour
    And with bitter hatred swell.

He had cast the thing most holy
    To the dogs ; before the swine
Pearls ; and for his noble rashness
    CÆSAR now must pay the fine.

In the garb of friendship vested,
    In petitioner's humble guise,
With the servile smile of falsehood
    Gleaming in their traitor eyes.

In the sacred hall of Council,
    Seated in his curule chair,

Fearless, trustful, in his own

Uprightness clothed, they stabbed him there.

At the base of Pompey's statue

Fell great Cæsar; but not waned

His star with him.   In world-wide Empire

Cæsar's work and name remained.

ST PAUL.[1]

FAREWELL, Rome. A nobler gospel
   Stirs my soul and shapes my song,
March of love divinely fervid,
   March of truth divinely strong.

I will sing a mighty marvel,
   How the lordly Roman drew
Fountain of new life pure-blooded
   From the mean unvalued Jew.

---

[1] "In Klopstock's 'Messiah,' the *truths*, the glorified facts being connected with more than historic belief, in the minds of men, the *fictions* came upon me like lies."—COLERIDGE, *Brandl.*, p. 364.

This has been my maxim throughout, specially with regard to St Paul.

How the Greek, the subtle-thoughted,
    With his cunning fence of wit,
At the feet of Hebrew teachers
    Learned with greedy ear to sit.

In Jerusalem's holy city,
    Where grave judgment loves to dwell,
Wisest of the seventy wise men,
    Sate the wise Gamaliel.

Near him sate a youth observant
    Of the wise words of the men,
Noting all their sharp decisions
    With quick ear and faithful pen,

SAUL of Tarsus. Short of stature,
    Slight of limb, and with an high-
Mounting forehead, and beneath
    Well-massed brows a piercing eye.

Quick to learn what statutes Moses
    Gave from God, and memoried well

In the best lore of the Talmud,
 Taught by wise Gamaliel.

Bold to plan and swift to venture,
 Counting danger for a jest,
When strong love, or mighty hatred,
 Flowed like spring-tide in his breast.

He had seen unlettered preachers
 Bred in Jesus' lowly school,
With a loose unlicensed doctrine
 Spurn the high priest's lawful rule.

He had seen its foremost spokesman
 With a death of heavy stoning,
For his rude-mouthed contradiction,
 Give the Law its due atoning.

And he vowed with words of fiery
 Vengeance, and with purpose fell,
In the holy city's cincture
 Nevermore such brood shall dwell.

And he chased them as a hunter
Chases with a keen-nosed hound,
To Gerizim, to Mount Tabor,
To Mount Hermon's utmost bound.

And he seized both men and women
Where the hated sect prevailed,
Old and young, and to the prison's
Gloomy den of durance haled.

And he journeyed to Damascus
In the fever of his wrath—
When, behold! a flash from Heaven
Flared across his blinded path.

And he heard a strange voice crying,
"SAUL, O SAUL! what moveth thee
With hot breath of persecution
Sharply thus to follow me?

"Rise, and get thee to Damascus;
Thou shalt learn there what to do.

Thine old life is dead.   My servant
   There shall shape thy course anew."

Paul hath hied him to Damascus,
   Where the white-walled splendour gleams
Through the wide-spread green, the dowry
   Of the many-branching streams.

He hath entered fair Damascus ;
   And the servant of the Lord
Touched him there with spirit-piercing
   Power of truth and healing word.

And he rose as one that riseth
   From long death, into a new
Stretch of blissful life, with warmer
   Pulse of love and larger view.

And he went into the desert,
   There with searching thought to pray
O'er the purpose of the Lord,
   That led him in a wondrous way.

And he looked, and with new eyes
   The inner soul of things he saw,
Soul of Right that for its service
   Brooketh fleshly forms of Law,

Forms of Law that wisely fetter
   Idle eye and wandering foot,
Till the bud grow to the blossom,
   Till the blossom grow to fruit.

Meats and drinks, and times and seasons,
   Feasts that wait upon the moon,
Prayers with formal iteration
   Conned at matin-bell or noon.

Sabbaths, washings, circumcisions,
   Sanctities that brush the skin,
Making clean the fleshly cover,
   Leaving foul the soul within.

Holy vestments fringed with Scripture,
   Hearts unholy big with pride,

And where widows' homes are plundered,
  Tithes and taxes multiplied.

All this 'fore his brooding spirit
  Passed in penitent review ;
And he cast old things behind him,
  And he leapt into the new.

In the queenly state of Antioch
  By Orontes' winding flood,
Here the new pure faith, firm rooted,
  First shot forth a lusty bud.

Thither Paul, divinely missioned,
  Came ; and holy brethren there
Sent him forth on wings of faith,
  The message of God's love to bear

To distant shores.   And first to Cyprus,
  Where the foam-born Paphian queen
Turned to shame the grace of beauty
  With unholy rites obscene.

There the high-souled Hebrew preacher
　　Swayed the wise proconsul's mind,
But with ban of condemnation
　　Smote the godless sorcerer blind.

Thence across Cilician waters,
　　O'er the rough Pisidian ridges,
Over cliffs that knew no pathway,
　　Over floods that knew no bridges.

By the haunts of thieves and robbers,
　　'Neath the scowling tempest's frown,
Lashed by scourge of persecution
　　From unfriendly town to town ;

Through a wide unwatered country,
　　Dreary slope and cheerless meadow,
On to Derbe, on to Lystra,
　　Where the black mount casts his shadow.

There the rude unlettered people,
　　Circling round to gaze on Paul,

When they saw a lame man leaping
　　At the preacher's potent call,

Deemed they saw a god—Mercurius—
　　Come to earth in mortal guise ;
And they came with ox and garlands,
　　And with smoke of sacrifice

Stood before him.　But with lofty-
　　Souled rebuke he raised his hand,
And named the God that owns all worship,
　　Lord of sky and sea and land.

Thence he passed on through Galatia,
　　Where the lewd unchastened priest
Serves the car-drawn mighty mother
　　Of each huge-maned tawny beast ;

And they heard his word with gladness,
　　And their carnal creed denied,
And new spirit-life within them
　　Sprang from Christ the crucified.

But now Europe claimed the preacher ;
   Touched by power of truth divine,
O'er the broad Ægean waters
   Greece must bow to Palestine.

Macedonia hailed his coming ;
   On Philippi's storied plains
Many a generous host received him,
   Unbound from unworthy chains.

On to Athens.   As a soldier
   Gladly goes where dangers wait,
So the wisest of the wise men
   Paul will front in high debate.

On the hill of Mars he met them,
   Where Athena's pillared shrine
Looks serenely o'er the gardened
   Wealth of olive and of vine.

There they flocked around him ; Stoics
   And a looser-girdled crew—

Sophists, rhetors, glib discoursers,
　With quick ears for something new.

What a hot-brained fool shall babble
　May amuse an hour to hear ;
Dreamful Jews are wisely answered,
　When a subtle Greek shall sneer.

Paul arose ; and " Men and brethren,"—
　Thus he spake,—" well known to me
Is your vague and wide-armed worship
　Of all idol gods that be.

" As I passed I saw an altar
　Scriptured to the god unknown ;
God is known in all His doings,
　God supreme, and God alone ;

" God who looks forth from the heavens,
　God whose love makes glad the earth,
God from whom this well-compacted
　Cosmos takes its wondrous birth ;

"God of whom we are the offspring,
    Common-blooded, great and small,
Breathing common breath that pulses
    Through the oneness of the All;

"God whom men do vainly shape
    As man in silver or in stone,
Broad as day, and wide as space,
    And in no human likeness shown.

"Him hath Christ His chosen prophet,
    Born of Hebrew seed, declared,
And in fulness of the ages
    His eternal counsel bared,

"That no longer with unchastened
    Fancy men may forge a lie,
Human gods to touch and handle,
    Gods to sell, and gods to buy.

"And now He commandeth all men
    With a reasonable faith

To receive as wise disciples
  What the God-sent teacher saith;

"Teacher promised long, and visioned
  In dim gleamings scantly shed,
Now revealed; and with miraculous
  Rising raised up from the dead;

"Raised, and on a throne high-seated,
  To be judge of all below,
Greek and Hebrew, bond and freeman,
  In the day that He doth know."

Thus he spake; some jeered, some doubted,
  Some denied; a noble few
Nursed the seed of truth that soon
  To world-wide green luxuriance grew.

Thence to Corinth. With unwearied
  Courier pace that spurns repose,
Where the sickliest sick are pining,
  There the good physician goes.

E

In the busy mart of nations,
  Pomp of art and golden splendour,
From the earthly Aphrodite
  He redeemed the gross offender.

Thence to Ephesus, where Diana,
  In her many-breasted pride,
From her many-pillared temple
  Flings her glamour far and wide.

There with still small voice of gospel
  Nobly true and simply wise,
He dispersed a drift of babblers
  Making merchandise of lies.

PAUL has conquered. In Europa,
  In rich Asia's fair domains,
Hoary Error feels a tremor
  Travelling through her fretful veins.

Priestly fear grim Superstition's
  Hasty-marching doom foretells,

Priestly venom in Jerusalem's
 Breast with sacred rancour swells.

Fearless, to the priestly city
 PAUL on pious quest doth go ;
There he stands with calm assurance,
 As a man that knows his foe.

With an oath of hellish hatred
 They have vowed to work his woe ;
He hath called for help to Cæsar,
 And to Cæsar he shall go.

O'er the treacherous Cretan waters,
 O'er the mid-sea's stormy roar,
Bound with fetters, heaped with slander,
 To Imperial Latium's shore

They have sent him.   He hath trodden
 The long Appian Way to Rome,
And beneath the Seven Hills' shelter
 Found a prison and a home.

But, as oft hath chanced, the tyrant
    Showed more mercy than the priest ;
Cæsar's truthful doom the true man
    From their net of lies released.

And he sped like an unpinioned
    Eagle to the extreme West,
Where Hispania's rocky barrier
    Flouts wide Ocean's billowy breast.

Westward, Eastward, never-resting,
    Like the rain, now here now there,
Bringing increase to the Churches
    Watered by his kindly care.

But the end was nigh.   The storm
    Lulled a moment, might not pass ;
Where he comes, strong hate comes with him,
    Snakes are lurking in the grass.

Rome beneath a monster-Cæsar
    Groans—brute, madman, devil, fool ;

Great men are a mark for murder
  Where a Nero bears the rule.

'Neath that hotbed of putrescence,
  Where Corruption grossly grew,
With the leaven of the Hebrew
  God was making all things new.

But the Old with stout persistence
  Revelled wildly in its shame,
And ramped through blood in heathen triumph
  O'er the hated Christian name.

Laws were loveless ; lies were blushless ;
  And the lust with feeding grew,
To glut the greed of wolf-nursed Rome
  With blood of Christian and of Jew.

PAUL was marked for doom.   Behold him
  On the bristling front of lies,
In the Prætor's hall of justice,
  Looking with untroubled eyes,

Hoping nought, and nothing fearing :
   Well he knew his hour was nigh,
Bravely schooled in face of foemen
   As a Christian dies to die.

Outside of the bloody city,
   Close by Caius Cestius' tomb,
On the road that leads to Ostia,
   There they marched him to his doom.

Through the streaming of the people
   Forth he marched, a motley crew,
Merchants, sailors, usurers, wondering
   At the calm front of the Jew.

To a grassy place they led him,
   Where three bubbling fountains flow,
O'er the dry growth of the summer
   Spreading freshness from below.

There they made a ring around him ;
And the headsman with a sword
Headless by the bubbling fountains
Laid the servant of the Lord.

CANTO II.

THE MIDDLE AGES

COLUMBA.

I WILL sing a song of heroes,
   When the ages rang the knell
Of the iron-hearted Rome,
   That like a palsied Titan fell.

Of that foul Ægean stable,
   Where the rank corruption grew,
Paul's sure word made sweeping clearance;
   Old things passed away, and new

Shot into life. I sing COLUMBA,
   Born far West in sea-girt home,
In the clovered green Ierne
   Named, not known, by mighty Rome.

God hath chosen the barbarian,
   Things unvalued, worthless, weak,
To abase the lordly Roman,
   To confound the subtle Greek.

Vainly had imperial rancour
   Like a sanguine deluge spread,
When the axe of Diocletian
   Severed Alban's holy head.

Vainly might the painted idols
   Bar from light their dark dominion ;
In the far Galwegian outland
   Rose the pure white shrine of Ninian.

Like the coming of the swallows,
   When sweet showers uncoil the fern,
Came a host of God-sent teachers,
   Serf, Palladius, Kentigern,

To redeem from heathen darkness
   All the roving Scots that be,

Where the huge-heaved Grampian bulwark
　Slopeth eastward to the sea.

To the fierce hot-blooded Erin
　Patrick brought the Gospel grace ;
But brawls and battles, feuds and factions,
　Swayed the old untempered race

Then, when Phelim's son far-venturing
　From the wooded hill of Derry,
Through the foamy Loch Foyle waters
　Northward sailed in wicker wherry.

For a ban was laid upon him,
　For that once in plunge of passion
He had drawn the sword of vengeance,
　In a hot unpriestly fashion,

At the battle of Culdreimhne,
　When from all the brave O'Neills
Diarmid and the men of Connaught
　Fled with terror at their heels.

Malise, priest of Innish Murry,
  On COLUMBA laid the ban,
Through Hebridean seas to voyage
  And convert the Pictish clan.

And with twelve high-souled companions
  He cut through the briny spray,
Till he came where whistling west winds
  Flout the front of Colonsay.

But not halted there ; for clearly,
  When the sun unveiled the morn,
Thence he saw the dear-loved Erin
  Which his chaste vow had forsworn.

Northward, northward, ever northward,
  Through the wild waves' tumbling roar,
Where through ragged drift of storm-cloud
  Frowned the dark cone of Ben More.

On he steered through heaving waters,
  Plash of waves, and windy roar,

Till he came to where Iona
  Steeply piles her southmost shore.

There no more might view of Erin
  Tempt his chaste eye to look back,
Tempt his heart with homeward longings
  To retrace the briny track.

There he moored his boat, his currach,
  In the lone rock-girdled bay,
Where with wondering eye the stranger
  Notes it fossiled in the clay.

Nor halted there, but for to breathe
  The landward air a little space :
Eastward then with foot unwearied
  He pursued the holy chase ;

For himself, and all that shared
  His brave apostleship, he bound
Not to rest till they should greet
  The Pictish king on Pictish ground.

Brude his name, whose heathen stronghold
   From a lofty seat looks forth,
Where the Ness his broad stream mingles
   With the salt sea of the North.

Northward now with foot unwearied
   O'er the granite ridge he sped,
Where Ben Nevis, king of mountains,
   Stoutly rears his massive head.

Up the steep cliffs, down the corrie,
   O'er the broad moor's purple breast,
Where link on link of sistered waters
   Join the North sea to the West.

Now he stands before Dun Phadraig,
   Where King Brude in shaggy state
Cinctured sits with hoary Druids,
   Brooding o'er the coming Fate.

Here he stands with saintly Congall
   And with Kenneth of Achaboe

Three in body, one in power,
　　To lay a host of demons low.

For the Druids worshipped demons,
　　Gods of earth and air and sky,
Peopling land and peopling water
　　With the glamour of a lie.

And with spells and incantations
　　They did bind the heart of Brude,
That he closed his gates against
　　The bearers of the holy rood.

Vainly ; saintly Congall lifted
　　High the virtue of the rood,
And from it flashed a light that smote
　　With blindness all the sorcerer brood.

And COLUMBA, with a potent
　　Voice like thunder rolling near,
Quelled the king's obdurate stoutness
　　With a thrill of holy fear.

F

For he sang a psalm that David[1]
    Wont to sing when he arose,
Girt with godlike strength, to prostrate
    The dread muster of his foes.

" We have heard it from our fathers,"—
    Thus he sang—no idle tale,—
" How the true God o'er the false gods
    Where He came did still prevail.

" How Thou didst cast out the heathen,
    And Thy people did prevail,
Not by sword and not by horses,
    Not by panoply of mail;

" But by Thy right arm, Jehovah,
    And by favour from above,
For that Thou didst hold Thy children
    In the strong embrace of love."

Thus he sang; and disenchanted
    From the Druid's spell, the king

---

[1] Psalm xliv. Vit. Columb., i. 29.

Open flung his oaken gates,
　And like a bird with folded wing

Bent the knee before COLUMBA,
　Kissed the rood uncrowned and bare :
And with water from the fountain
　Gladly they baptised him there.

And he rose with brave assurance,
　And he told his people all
From the demons' thrall to loose them
　At COLUMBA's saintly call.

And he gave the saint the island
　Where he landed for his dower,
There to work in sacred college
　God's soul-healing work with power.

In an age of rude-armed rapine,
　Feuds and wars without release,
There the saintly son of Phelim
　Taught the gentle arts of peace.

There he led the prattling mill-stream,
　There he drained the miry bog,
There he wove the wattled cabin,
　Hewed the tree and piled the log.

There with spade and hoe and mattock
　He laid bare Earth's fruitful breast,
To the wooing of the breezes
　Wafted from the genial West.

Oats he reaped and healthful barley
　Where the grass once sourly grew,
And where prickly furze was rampant
　Apple-blossoms came to view.

Honey pilfered from the heather
　Wisely in warm hives he stored ;
Milk and eggs and fish supplied
　Chaste feeding to his sober board.

But with spirit-nurture chiefly
　There were fed the saintly men,

Chaunting psalms of holy David,
　Writing with a faithful pen.

Evermore at nones and vespers,
　Evermore at matin chime,
They made sweet their souls with music
　From pure text and holy rhyme.

And they did their tale of doing,
　Each man to his function true,
With ungrudging sweet obedience
　To high-saintly wisdom due;

Where the strong man helped the weak man,
　And the weak man loved the strong,
And brothered work with work was mingled
　Like sweet notes in cunning song.

And the old men taught the young men,
　Nicely reared in learnèd school,
To subdue the lawless-roving
　Heathen to the Christian rule.

Thirty years and four he taught them,
   Sent them missioned o'er the sea,
Sent them southward to Bernicia,
   Sent them northward to Maree.

Then as good men die he died,
   Shedding smiles and blessings round,
At the solemn hour of midnight
   Kneeling upon holy ground,

With sweet text from well-conned psalter
   In his memory wisely stored,
" No good thing shall e'er be wanting
   To His saints that seek the Lord."

There he knelt before the altar,
   All alone with God in prayer ;
And he raised his eyes to heaven,
   And beheld in vision fair

Angel-faces sweetly beckoning,
   And he heard with raptured ear

David's song of liberation
  Angel-voices hymning near.

And a glory from the altar
  Shone ; the church was filled with light,
And the white-smocked brethren saw it
  Gleaming through the hazy night.

And they rushed into the holy
  Presence of the prayerful man,
Where he lay with sideward-drooping
  Head, and visage pale and wan.

And with gentle hands they raised him,
  And he mildly looked around,
And he raised his arm to bless them,
  But it dropped upon the ground.

And his breathless body rested
  On the arms that held him dear,
And his dead face looked upon them
  With a light serene and clear.

And they said that holy angels
  Surely hovered round his head,
For alive no loveliest ever
  Looked so lovely as this dead.

ALFRED.

I WILL sing of Saxon ALFRED,
  ALFRED, king, and clerk, and bard :
Triple name, and triple glory,
  By no stain of baseness marred.

Blood of Cerdic, blood of Ine,
  Blood of Egbert in his veins ;
Reaper of the past, and sower
  Of the future, ALFRED reigns.

Mighty England, queen of peoples,
  Slept well-cradled in his breast,
Grew to world-wide reach of lordship
  From the Saxon of the West.

'Mid the leafy wealth of Berkshire
  Oak and beech in breezy play,
'Mid green England's gardened beauty,
  Up he shot into the day ;

Shot and rose, and grew to youthhood,
  'Neath a mother's gentle care,
Osburh, with a soul as kindly
  As the balmy summer air.

And he sat and breathed her sweetness,
  And he drank with greedy ear
Tales of old ancestral glory,
  When no plundering Danes were near.

And his heart did beat accordant,
  And his eye with joy did swell,
When with mother's love she mingled
  Matin chant and vesper bell.

Keen to learn and quick was ALFRED,
  From a song or from a book ;

Never slow to catch the meaning
   Of a gesture or a look.

Like wise bird that flits about,
   Linnet, finch, or crow, or sparrow,
Pecking seed with lively beak,
   From brown track of hoe or harrow ;

Or like fruitful honey-bee
   In bright glow of summer weather,
Wise the thorny spray to plunder,
   Or the tufts of purple heather.

Mild was ALFRED as a maiden ;
   But with soul untaught to fear,
He, in Hubert's craft the foremost,
   Lanced the boar and chased the deer.

Nor in breezy forest only
   Grew, and kind embrace of home,
But with wondering eye young ALFRED
   Saw the pomp of mighty Rome.

And with wider view grew wider,
　　And more wise with vagrant ken,
What to shun and what to gather
　　From the works of diverse men.

Thus the youth ; but storms were brewing
　　From the rude sea-roving clan,
Storms to front with manly stoutness,
　　When the youth should be a man.

Drifting as a grey blast drifteth
　　From the sharp and biting East,
Growing with the greed of plunder,
　　Ever as their spoil increased,

Came the Northmen.　Where the waters
　　Of the Ouse, ship-bearing, sweep
Round the palace of the Cæsars ;
　　Where on Durham's templed steep

Learnèd Bede and saintly Cuthbert
　　Slept in keep of holy men ;

Where the toilful monks of Croyland
　　Clave the clod and drained the fen,

Honest work and sacred uses
　　Trampling under foot profane,
Revelling in blood and murder,
　　Lust and rapine, came the Dane.

On the sunny slope of Bury,
　　Where the fruitful fields are spread,
From its trunk the savage Ingvar
　　Severed Edmund's holy head.

Westward then the sea-kings drifted;
　　Thames with gentle-flowing water
Shrank perturbed, and castled Reading
　　Wept o'er fields of crimson slaughter.

Fear smote bravest hearts; but ALFRED,
　　With the young man's pride of daring,
Scaled the bristling steep of Ashdown,
　　Fined them there with loss unsparing.

Bravely he ; but as in spring-time,
　Big with ever new supplies,
Widely spread the snow-fed waters
　O'er the green embankment rise,

So the Vampires of the North Sea,
　Self-recruited more and more,
Sweep with swelling devastation
　All the vexed Devonian shore.

But the hunted beast finds shelter.
　ALFRED fled, but might not yield ;
In a tangled maze of marshes,
　Westmost Somerset did shield

England's saviour.　Lurking lowly
　With the lowliest in the land,
There, a cowherd with the cowherds,
　And a scanty faithful band,

Feeding pigs with roots and acorns,
　Wandering in poor harper's guise,

For God's hour of sure redemption
ALFRED waits with faithful eyes.

With his mother's saintly lessons,
    With King David's holy psalm,
'Mid the swell and roar of danger
    He doth keep his spirit calm.

God-sent visions cheered his slumbers;
    Holy Cuthbert, from the Tyne,
Came and filled with bread his basket,
    Filled his scanted cup with wine.

Fenced with bristling wood and marshes,
    In the isle of Athelney,
Where the creeping stream disputes
    Its doubtful border with the sea:

There he lurked; and there he waited
    Till the favouring hour; and then,
At his call the golden dragon,
    Over forest, moor, and fen,

To the reborn strength of Wessex
    Spread its wing.[1]   With heavy loss,
At Ethandune, the savage Viking
    Bit the ground, and kissed the cross.[2]

ALFRED now is king indeed—
    King as few great kings may be;
He hath gained his crown by labour,
    He hath set his people free.

With a heart that never fainted,
    With a faith that never failed,
With an eye that watched and waited,
    With a strong arm that prevailed,

He hath fought and conquered.   Now,
    What remains for him to do?
What the great man ever doeth,
    From the old to shape the new:

---

[1] The golden dragon was the ancient banner of Wessex.—
Pauli, Life of Alfred, p. 51.

[2] Guthorm, the Danish king, actually embraced Christi-
anity.—Ibid., p. 182.

Not by forceful harsh uprooting,
   But with gently guiding hand,
As a father guides his children,
   Spreading union through the land.

Stern decree and kindly caring
   Turned rude souls to loyal awe ;
Christ and Moses, nicely blended,
   Swayed his soul and shaped his law.

If a poor man feared a rich man,
   He might knock at ALFRED's gate ;
If a rich man wronged a poor man,
   He must fear a felon's fate.

If you hung a golden bracelet
   By the road in ALFRED's time,
No rude hand might dare remove it,
   Such sure vengeance followed crime.

Nor alone with finely-feeling
   Touch he swayed the pulse of home,

But leagued with kings beyond the Channel,
  And the sacred state of Rome,

Eastward far to broad-streamed Indus
  Saxon ALFRED's greeting came,
And the remnant of St Thomas
  Hailed the omen of his name.

But not like the Macedonian,
  ALFRED triumphed with the sword;
O'er the scholar's book of learning
  He with pious patience pored.

Well he knew that of all noble
  Doing Thought is rightful lord;
And the pen indites the wisdom
  That gives honour to the sword.

With a ring of learnèd clerics
  He embraced his kingly throne,
And their wisdom, freely subject,
  Paid rich tribute to his own.

As a wise physician gathers
    Healing herbs from field and shore,
So from Saxon books and Latin
    ALFRED swelled his thoughtful store.

Seeking far and searching deeply,
    Everywhere he culled the best;
Gospel grace and Stoic sentence
    Warmed his heart and mailed his breast.

From the Pope and from the Pagan,
    Greekish school and monkish college,
Where the seed of truth was scattered,
    ALFRED reaped the crop of knowledge;

Reaped the lore of all that hated
    Darkness, all that loved the light,
All that called him England's darling,
    Champion of the Saxon right.

But the sky of kings is never
    Long from troublous clouding clear;

Evermore some gathered thunder
    Taints the summer joy with fear.

Once again the sea-marauders
    Dashed his cup of bliss with bale,
And the Viking oared his galleys
    Up the tide of Kentish Swale.

Westward by sun-fronting Devon,
    Where the Land's End flouts the main,
Up fair Bristol's tideful channel,
    Winged with ruin came the Dane.

Strong-walled Chester knew their terror,
    High-ridged Cambria bowed her head,
Where in pride of devastation
    Hasting came with iron tread.

But as some old oak-tree grandly
    Stands amid the crashing wood,
Rooted in the strength of ALFRED
    Stout old Wessex bravely stood.

He who wars with foxes, fox-like
 Must devise the needful wile;
On the sea to meet the sea-king
 Alfred knew by Vectis' isle.

Sixty-oared he made his galleys,
 England's navy in the germ,
And the sea-king's wingèd pinnace
 With unwonted swift alarm

Fled from Vectis. England now
 Breathed with full lungs free from fear;
Nor again in face of Alfred
 Might the plundering Dane appear.

Eastward where old Thames majestic
 Laves the fort of stout King Lud,
Westward where the bluff-faced granite
 Mocks old Ocean's fretful flood,

Alfred looked : and all around him,
 Once a field of wasteful strife,

Saw the land redeemed from wildness
  By the labour of his life ;

Saw, and thanked his God ; then laid him
  Down to sleep, and down to die,
Finished with the earthly, ready
  For new launch of life on high.

WALLACE AND BRUCE.

I will sing of Bruce and Wallace,
  Sons of Jove to help our need,
Then when Norman Edward lusted
  For wide sway benorth the Tweed.

Doughty robbers were the Normans,
  In rude rapine born and bred,
Bold as lion, fierce as tiger,
  When they came with iron tread,

And with subtle fox-like wisdom,
  Wise to weave a web of lies,
Where a lie might seem the shortest
  Way to snatch a glittering prize.

English Edward from the Norman
　　Drew his state, and drew his blood,
Drew the despot-lust to trample
　　All free manhood in the mud.

When he found a stout gainsayer,
　　He would hang him for a knave ;
When he found a weakling, he
　　Would gild the chain that bound the slave.

And he grew up with keen hunger
　　Of more land to swell his state ;
And he forged the name of Scotland
　　In proud England's book of Fate.

'Tis the logic of all robbers,
　　Romans, Normans, to make better
What they steal, and let the weak man
　　Wisely wear the strong man's fetter.

When the good King Alexander,
　　Who made haughty Haco mourn,

Fell, to find a briny burial,
  From the steep cliff of Kinghorn;

When the Maiden-queen from Norway
  Sailed and sickened on the sea,
And the crown without a wearer
  Waited where the right might be,

Scotland lay defenceless, headless;
  Then the robber knew his hour,
Like a hawk upon the pigeons
  Down to swoop, and to devour.

With a train of clerks and lawyers,
  And a venal Romish scribe,
To the castled steep of Norham
  Edward came, with craft to bribe

Any basest Scottish lordling,
  Norman-bred, that would kneel down,
Swearing fealty to a swindler
  For the bauble of a crown.

Baliol took the bribe, as Clio,
  Just recorder, set it down,
BALIOL REIGNS, THE TRAITOR-SLAVE,
  WHO SOLD HIS PEOPLE FOR A CROWN.

He shall lick the foot that kicked him,
  And with service cringing low,
He shall swallow down the spittle
  Of his high contemptuous foe.

At Strathcathro, at Strathcathro,
  Whelmed with shame and swift disaster,
He shall kiss the clay bare-headed,
  And from England's haughty master

Beg his craven life. The crafty
  Longshanks now had played his game,
And Cimbric Wales and Celtic Albyn
  Bowed before the Norman name,

To his deeming. But there wanted
  Much to make his deeming true ;

He had juggled, not the people,
  But a vile and venal crew,

Norman-bred, half-hearted lordlings,
  Dangling round a stranger throne ;
But the people prayed and waited
  For a leader of their own ;

And God sent him. WILLIAM WALLACE,
  Starred with no heraldic pride,
But with proof of thews and sinews,
  From the bosom of Strathclyde

Rose, a Scot with blood untainted,
  And with heart unbribed to stand
Stoutly 'gainst a thousand Edwards,
  For the honour of the land.

Sooth, he was a man to look to
  In an hour of danger ; tall,
Strong, broad-shouldered, well-compacted,
  Grandly furnished forth with all

That makes a man a man; in action
   Bold; in speech persuasive, mild,
Mingling firm stern-purposed manhood
   With the sweetness of a child.

And like Moses, quick to feel,
   And nothing slow to strike was he,
When he laid the insolent Selby
   Breathless in the fair Dundee.

And the minions of the Percy,
   When he fished in Irvine water,
Spoilers of his scaly booty,
   He sent home to tell of slaughter.

In the castled strength of Lanark,
   Where they killed his bonnie bride,
Many a haughty Norman hireling
   With their heart's blood stained the Clyde.

Tremble, Edward, for thy lordship;
   When thy pride usurped a throne,

WALLACE wight with Scotland's freemen
Drove thy titled slave from Scone.

Aberdonia, granite-fronted,
  Strong Dunottar by the sea,
Perth fair-meadowed, tall-towered Brechin,
  Shook the fetters from the free.

In the pride of kingship, Edward
  Sent the creatures of his will,
Belted priests and knights of prowess,
  Trained in war and tactic skill,

Sheer to death to hunt the WALLACE ;
  But the WALLACE from the Tay
Marched with thunder-pace, and smote
  Their serried ranks with sore dismay,

'Neath the castled steep of Stirling,
  Where the Forth with fruitful pride
Round the cloistered Cambuskenneth
  Slowly rolls its mossy tide.

Like a troop of deer they hurried,
   Spurred by fear, with rattling speed,
Till the near-seen England cheered them
   From the forted banks of Tweed !

Scotland now might breathe; but only
   For a space; her traitor lords,
Norman-bred and Norman-blooded,
   Drooped their crests and sheathed their swords

To the proud usurper's summons,
   Who, to tyrant wisdom true,
Marched with well-massed weight of numbers,
   To down-tramp the patriot few.

On the far-viewed heights of Falkirk,
   There his bristling lines he drew ;
There with sweep of circling thousands
   He outwinged the faithful few.

Victor he ; but vanquished WALLACE
   Beaten stood, not broken ; he

In the deep heart of the people
  Reigned the free king of the free.

Wisely from the strife a season
  He withdrew, and sought in France
And in Rome a strong assertor
  Of his rightful-wielded lance.

But the strong-willed fierce invader,
  Year by year his wasteful course
Followed, till high-forted Stirling
  Fell before his battering force ;

Fell, and bowed the head to England.
  Only one man's head stood high,
WALLACE, for his truth to Scotland
  Marked for death by Edward's eye ;

Marked for death by traitor lordlings,
  By the false Menteith, who sold
Scotland's grace and Scotland's honour
  For a bag of English gold.

To great London town they haled him,
　　Tried him there in mock of right,
Doomed him to the death of felons,
　　Gibbeted in public sight.

And the haughty harsh usurper,
　　With a cold unfeeling eye,
Drawn and quartered, disembowelled,
　　Saw the noblest Scotsman die.

Edward now had dreamless slumber,
　　None might mock his purple state;
Like a dog with gilded collar,
　　Scotland watched at England's gate;

Or like a dog for hunting cherished,
　　Fed on bones from groaning board,
That his life may do good service,
　　Nosing game to feed his lord.

Might had triumphed for the moment,
　　But the Fates can bide their time ;
Slow and sure the God-sent Fury
　　Follows on the track of crime.

'Mid the pomp of Edward's palace,
　　With the servile Norman crew,
BRUCE had nursed in faithful memory
　　Scotland's crown to Scotland due.

Not, like WALLACE, pure ; but tainted
　　With the breath of courts and kings,
To his country, late-repentant,
　　Loyal heart and sword he brings.

On the bridge of busy London
　　He had seen a ghastly sight—
Norman foplings staring, jeering,
　　At the head of WALLACE wight.

And he felt as one that basely
　　Had forsworn his natal right,

And for gleam of courtly favour
　　Bowed his head to lawless might.

And as Paul, who erst had goaded
　　To the death the Christian clan,
Came new-fashioned to Damascus,
　　And to blessing changed his ban ;

So from London to Lochmaben
　　Came the BRUCE a reborn man,
For his crown and for his country
　　To fight nobly in the van ;

To the seat of royal Kenneth,
　　Where the thanes, with glad acclaim,
Crowned him Robert King of Scotland,
　　Freed from England's yoke of shame.

Like a bolt from Jove on Edward
　　Flashed the fact—"King crowned at Scone!"
On the seat of the MacAlpine,
　　Whence he stole the fateful stone.

Nevermore might Edward brook it ;
  He had boldly robbed and won,
Like a Roman, like a Norman ;
  Could such proud work be undone ?

Up he rose in wrath Titanic ;
  Like a white squall on the sea,
Like a vulture keen for carrion,
  Down on Scottish land swooped he.

Methven knew his scathful scourging,
  Almond water flowed with blood ;
Rough Glendochart's rocky current,
  Far Loch Awe's long-gleaming flood,

Saw the rightful monarch hounded
  By the proud usurper's host ;
Many bravest fell around him,
  But he stood, and stoutly crossed

Swords with three, and lifeless laid them
  'Twixt the Loch-side and the brae,

Where the false MacDougal vainly
    Strove to block his kingly way.

But his way might not be southward—
    Pembroke now held all the plain;
He must watch and wait in hardship
    Till the good hour come again.

Fortune will be wooed with patience;
    Never mortal man was great
In the evil hour who knew not
    How to suffer and to wait.

With the Douglas, with the Campbell,
    By Loch Lomond, in Cantire,
In peaked Arran's rocky cincture,
    Nursing Scotland's heart's-desire,

For the ripening hour of judgment
    BRUCE did bravely wait and bear,
While the victor, tiger-hearted,
    Valiant knights and ladies fair

Chained and caged, and made the scaffold
  Glib with blood of noble men.
In his native wilds of Carrick,
  Like a beast from den to den

Hunted, BRUCE, with never-failing,
  Stout, high-purposed faith, did stand
Dauntless, with a loyal-hearted
  Few, for honour of the land.

Once there came of grim Galwegians
  Twice a hundred men to hound him ;
All alone, beside a boggy,
  Black, slow-winding stream they found him.

But he stood as stands a lion
  Strong before a barking dog ;
And twice five and four he stretched them
  Breathless on the crimsoned bog.

Then he marched against the Pembroke's
  Host, well massed with ordered skill ;

But their plunging steeds were shattered
On his spears at Loudon Hill.

Woe to Edward! he had trampled
On the bleeding worm, the Scot :
But the worm, the hydra-headed,
Should have died, but die would not.

To Carlisle, all fretful fuming,
Down he shot, the Scots to hammer;
But o'er his eye with vengeance flashing
Fate had spread a deathful glamour.

And he died on Solway, breathing
Curses on the Scottish clan;
But He did laugh who sits in heaven,
And into blessing changed the ban.

Edward died; but not with him
Died his fell and forceful doing;

With the heirship of his rancour,
Edward's Edward rushed to ruin.

Like a bird uncaged from durance,
    Bruce now spread his ampler wing ;
Inverness and granite-fronted
    Aberdonia hailed him king.

Rose the cry from eastmost Buchan,
    Here no Norman lord we know !
Swelled from central Perth the slogan,
    Lay the proud usurper low !

Through the breadth of Selkirk forest,
    With red blood from English slaughter
Gallant Douglas stained the tide
    Of Ettrick's mountain-girdled water.

Scotland too could boast her Edward,
    Brothered to King Robert ; he
Loose as mist the vauntful St John
    Drave from granite banks of Cree.

At the base of tway-peaked Cruachan,
　　John of Lorn was clothed with shame ;
And thy sea-fronting hold, Dunstaffnage,
　　Hailed the BRUCE with loud acclaim.

Nor the sword alone was loyal,
　　But on heights of fair Dundee
All the crosier-bearing people
　　Signed a bond to Scotland free.

At Linlithgow, dear to story,
　　Eight men from a wain of hay
Leapt, and like a drift of pigeons
　　Drave the Normans in deray.

Not thy castled strength, Dunedin,
　　Fearless now might front the sky,
There where on thy steepest steepness
　　Randolph cast his daring eye.

And he clomb with slippery venture,
　　As a sailor climbs a rope,

Leapt the wall, and drave the warders
  Hurrying down the eastern slope.

Stroke on stroke, as near and nearer
  Marched the God-predestined time,
When the son should answer prostrate
  For the father's lofty crime.

Southward from high-forted Stirling
  Flows a brook, slow-winding, through
Boggy meads and ragged fringes,
  'Neath green slopes of ample view.

There the BRUCE with wise disposal
  Massed his men in order fair ;
Gallant Randolph, Keith, and Douglas,
  Sworn to death or victory there.

Wisely too with cunning foresight,
  Where the foeman's charge would be,
Pits he dug, and stakes he planted,
  Roofed with grass that none might see.

'Twas a bright June day ; and each man
   On the fragrant grassy sod
Knelt at holy mass devoutly,
   And confessed his sins to God.

Onward came the banded foemen,
   Flashing, dashing, horse and man,
Norman, Gascon, Welsh, and Irish,
   Brave De Bohun in the van.

Like an eagle proudly swooping
   From Jove's chair on stormy wing,
On he rushed, with lance hot thirsting
   For the blood of Scotland's king.

But the king, who wore the bonnet,
   Rose, and with a mighty strain
Hove his battle-axe, and sheerly
   Clave the knight through helm and brain.

Well begun is half well-ended,
   Nor the fight may linger long

Where the free man fights for freedom,
And the strong man leads the strong.

On the mailèd Norman riders
  Charged, in clattering multitude ;
But the Scots with steady frontage
  Like a bristling forest stood.

Valiant Keith, the doughty marshal,
  With five hundred knights in mail,
Prostrate laid the English archers,
  As corn falls before the hail.

Heavenward rose the Scottish slogan,
  While the gillies on the hill,
Spreading show of sheets for banners,
  Downward rushed with forward will ;

Which the fear-struck, far beholding,
  Fled like children from a ghost ;
And their king, with floating bridle,
  Galloped from the dwindling host.

Forth and Bannock drank the red blood
Of ten times ten thousand slain ;
Who escaped, like chaff were drifted
Where the west wind sweeps the plain.

Edward's Edward, shorn of kingship,
Fled the land and found the sea ;
From Dunbar a light skiff brought him
Where his breathing might be free ;

Even as Xerxes, cowed and crestless,
Backward ploughed fair Helle's tide,
Reaping, as the proud man reapeth,
Lowest fall from topmost pride.

Fought and won is Freedom's battle ;
Scotland's Muse no more shall mourn ;
England no more toss her haughty
Crest o'er glorious Bannockburn.

CANTO III.

THE NEW WORLD

LUTHER.

I WILL sing of Saxon LUTHER,
   Who from lowly peasant-home,
With brave word of truth forth-thundered,
   Shook the throne of mighty Rome.

Not for sway of sceptred Pontiffs,
   Gilded pomp, and purple pride,
High-poised domes and painted porches,
   Christ had lived and Christ had died.

Not the great and not the mighty,
   Not the lords of princely hall,
But the mean unvalued people,
   Answered to His holy call.

Not the churchman, not the learnèd
  Rabbis felt a Saviour's need,
In the lofty pride of station,
  In the nice conceit of creed.

Not for crowns and not for kingdoms
  Soldier Paul went forth to fight,
With the sharp sword of the Spirit,
  In the banded world's despite;

But for truth, and for redemption
  From crude faiths and fancies odd,
And for love to all who own
  A common fatherhood in God.

But old times were gone.   The bishop
  Now on Cæsar's earthly throne
Sate, and lust of domination
  Crept into him, blood and bone;

Lust of wealth and lust of splendour,
  And the charm in priestly eyes

To be worshipped by the millions
For a god in mortal guise;

And the lust of sacred wrath,
To hurl the thunderbolt of ban
On who dared with contradiction
To confront the mitred clan;

And the lust with mighty Cæsars
To conspire for forceful deed,
Or to lie with subtle statesmen
When a lie might serve the need.

God was mocked in His own temple:
When their sin was at full tide,
He prepared a Saxon miner's
Son to lop their mounting pride.

Little LUTHER little fancied
Such high honour on his head,
When he made the rounds at Eisenach,
Singing Christmas hymns for bread.

I

But the poor street-boy had broodings,
  Books he loved, and lute and lyre,
And beneath a breast of hardship
  Nursed a holy glowing fire ;

Holy fear, and holy reverence
  For the voice that speaks within ;
Holy fear of God, that judgeth
  Sinners self-condemned in sin ;

Fears of death, that in a moment
  Might strike down a guilty head :
By such holy terrors haunted,
  From the bustling world he fled

Into cloistered life at Erfurt ;
  Thence was called to learnèd school,
O'er the high-souled youth of Deutschland
  There to bear high-thoughted rule';

There to teach to prince and people,
  Not trite lessons of the hour,

But with flaming inspiration,
　　And with touch of Spirit-power.

And they held him high in honour,
　　And they missioned him to Rome,
There to see strange sights undreamt of
　　In his honest German home ;

There to see a swearing Pontiff,
　　Jesters dressed in priestly guise,
Monks with luxury bloated, bishops
　　Juggling souls with holy lies.

And he saw with sacred shudder
　　Dark-stoled salesmen, blushless, bold,
Selling grace of God for silver,
　　Opening gates of heaven for gold.

And he came back to his teaching,
　　Far from purple sins to dwell ;
And he preached to Saxon princes,
　　" Surely Rome is built on hell."

Tetzel came, a monk with red cross;
  In the market-place he stood,
Vending pardons by the sixpence
  To a gaping multitude.

In the market-place at Wittenberg
  High he stood, and lit a fire
To consume all bold protesters
  Who should cross the Pope's desire.

LUTHER heard—not made for skulking
  When a lie parades the street,
When the feeder of the people
  Vends a tainted drug for meat—

And he rose; and as a prophet,
  Fearing none but God on high,
Planted words of strong denial
  Boldly, in the public eye,

On the church door, five-and-ninety.
  Truth is mighty, and it spread

Like the blazing furze in summer,
 Like a voice that wakes the dead.

Leo heard it in his palace ;
 Tetzel heard, and foamed with ire,
And at Frankfurt flung the truthful
 Witness in the public fire.

He too marshalled forth his sentence,
 Blushless prophet of a lie,
And would plant his strong denial
 Boldly in the public eye.

But the students, with young heart's blood
 Boiling hot and mounting high,
'Mid the market throngs applausive,
 Burnt them in the public eye.

Trembled Leo in his palace,
 Trembled while he seemed to jest,
Humming tunes and twirling verses,
 With no churchly cares oppressed.

And he missioned glib discoursers,
   Legates, sophists, doctors, bred
In the school of high-conceited
   Insolence, with fatness fed.

And he hurled a ban against him,
   Puny creature of the clod,
Launching bolts of mimic thunder
   In the mimic name of God!

Foolish Pope! that boastful ban
   Is paper, nothing more, which brings
Fear to none who claims his right
   Of thinking from the King of kings.

All your marshalled pomp of curses,
   Blastful swell of priestly ban,
Like a whiff of breath it passes
   O'er the free soul of a Man.

LUTHER brought his troop together,
   Men with learnèd cap and gown,

Teachers and the taught together,
    To the east gate of the town.

And they piled a heap of fagots,
    And at touch of torch the flame
Rose ; and forward to the crackling
    Pile the bold monk gravely came.

In his hand the false Decretals
    And the big-mouthed boastful Bull,
Priest-made laws, and subtle dogmas
    Of an empty-witted school.

And to the flame he freely gave them,
    And he said with solemn cheer,
" *Let the wrath of God consume them*
    As this flame consumes them here !

" Canon law and false Decretals !
    Long, too long have lies prevailed—
Tiger-hearted, cruel monsters,
    Baby-brained and serpent-tailed ! "

And loud echoes rose applausive,
   And at Wittenberg each man
Freely breathed that day, rejoicing
   O'er the ashes of the ban.

Bulls are cindered, Popes are scouted ;
   What shall startled Europe do?
Let the holy Roman Cæsar
   Calm the strife with judgment true.

Charles hath come to Worms ; and with him
   His great lords in courtly show,
Waiting on his high decision,
   Big with mighty weal or woe !

LUTHER comes : no fear might hold him,
   Not the deathful shadow cast
From plotting priests and perjured kaisers
   In the memory of the past.

Rome had seen the axe of Nero
   Red with blood of holy Paul ;

Constance taught that oaths were worthless
   When Popes bribed the judgment-hall.

LUTHER came : it might rain devils ;
   Devils bring no fear to him ;
In the drowning of a world,
   He who trusts in God will swim.

LUTHER stands before the Kaiser :
   In the power of truth, that day,
Stood the miner's son of Mansfeld
   Mildly firm, nor knew dismay,

'Fore the banded might of princes,
   'Fore the purple Pope's array,
Stamping lies with name of Jesus,
   With red murder in their pay.

There he stood, like Paul when Nero
   Fixed on him his hangman's eye,
Ready for all fiery torture,
   But not ready for a lie.

Sooner would he swear that night
   Was day, and flout the front of fact,
Than of God's truth, in God's eye spoken,
   One smallest honest word retract.

Fumed the priest, and lowered the legate;
   LUTHER heard his sure death-knell,
" *Let the fire consume his body,*
   As his soul shall burn in hell! "
      .

But Charles was young, and Charles was prudent;
   Worms might milder show than Rome:
So he gave half-hearted licence,
   And brave LUTHER wandered home.

But a ban was sent behind him,
   That he breathed his breath in fear,
Doomed to wander, marked for judgment,
   With a lurking terror near.

But God keeps watch o'er His prophets.
   He had friends; and they, not blind,

From the ambushed murder snatched him,
   And in kindly ward confined

High upon the castled Wartburg:
   There his soul had time to brood
For what end the Lord had caught him
   From the murtherous multitude.

There he prayed and there he doubted,
   Doubted, prayed, and prayed again,
Tossed on sleepless pillow, doubting
   If his life had been in vain;

Doubting if he should not rather
   Break the shell of his disguise,
And face to face in deadly grapple
   Perish as a brave man dies;

By a host of terrors haunted,
   Demons mocking in despite,
Heaven close barred, and hell wide gaping,
   As he floundered through the night.

" *De profundis, De profundis!*
   Hear, dear God, O hear my cry!"
And a voice came through his slumber
   With an answer from on high:

" Take the Book; the Book shall help thee;
   Teach thy folk to read and think:
Priests may fight with axe and fagot;
   Thou shalt gain with pen and ink."

LUTHER rose, new-born, from slumber,
   Vanished clean all shapes of fear,
Braced for battle like a soldier,
   And he saw his mission clear.

Give the Book, the Book to all men,
   Let them see God face to face,
Let them hear the words of healing,
   Let them drink the well of grace.

From no priest that mumbles Latin
   With dumb gesture and grimace,

Tinkling bells, and smoking incense
    To becloud the holy place,

But from God's own mouth, or prophet's
    Clearly signed with faithful pen,
They shall hear God's word to Germans
    In the speech of German men !

Here was work, and here was plainly
    What the Lord would have him do ;
Better here to write and ponder,
    Than abroad, in public view,

Talking, wrangling, and disputing
    With a school-bred sophist crew
Using sleight of logic deftly
    Into false to twist the true.

And he worked with pious patience,
    As a German loves to plod,
Strong in lexicon and grammar,
    Till he sent the Word of God,

In its primal strength and freshness,
　　Full of quickening spirit-power,
To bring forth the Gospel seed-time
　　From the ferment of the hour.

And he sent it forth electric,
　　And it travelled like the fire,
Through the heart and through the pulsing
　　Veins, to reach the heart's desire,

Till the Council of the Princes,
　　Each man master in his home,
Doffed the badge of base subjection
　　To usurping priests in Rome;

Recking not if Popes might bluster,
　　Legates rage both North and South;
In the Book, the Book, were written
　　Words that gagged each boaster's mouth;

Recking not if witless weavers,
　　Or hot doctors of the school,

With a self-blown inspiration,
  Scorned the rein of healthy rule.

They had God's Book for their teacher,
  They had LUTHER for their guide ;
And he came with fervid shrewdness
  To rebuke the windy pride

Of each brainless preaching braggart.
  And the word of soundness grew,
And new thousands mustered daily,
  Swore allegiance to the true.

Popes were raging ; kings and kaisers
  Counsel took against the Lord ;
But the Book, the Book was stronger
  Than the crosier and the sword.

Wars had been, and wars were brewing—
  War and strife will ever be ;
But the truth of God will triumph
  When the Word of God is free.

LUTHER triumphed with the Bible;
And the Bible, now as then,
Peals the knell of death to despots,
Peals the psalm of life to men.

CROMWELL

I WILL sing of English OLIVER,
 Who, when kings were led by fools,
Led by fools, and served by brainless
 Pedants trained in priestly schools,

When the ship of State was tossing,
 And the storm-wings were abroad,
Seized the helm and gave it guidance,
 With a right direct from God.

Not in softly-curtained cradles
 Kings are nursed who claim from God,
But in labour's school He trains them,
 And He lifts them from the sod.

K

In the marshes of the Eastland,
   Where the gently-gliding Ouse
Creeps through fringe of sedge and willow,
   Grew the boy whom God did choose.

Erect he grew, of goodly stature,
   With strong limbs well knit together,
And stout ruddy cheeks that borrowed
   Freshness from the breezy weather.

As a yeoman's son might well be,
   Manly-browed with flowing hair,
Nose of power, and eyebrows shaggy,
   With keen lightnings lurking there.

Hot was he for bold adventure,
   Quick to share the riskful joy,
When a dovecot or an orchard
   Tempted any daring boy.

But not merely in the dash
   Of venture he would lead the van ;

Thoughts of mighty mark grew with him,
  As the boy grew to the man.

Oft at evening you might find him
  Pacing by the grassy fen,
Pondering o'er God's mystic counsel,
  And the tangled ways of men ;

Brooding o'er life's strange enigma,
  Spirit mingled with the clay,
Devils wrestling with good angels
  For the young heart's doubtful sway.

There he brooded, prayed and pondered,
  O'er the passioned yeast within,
Till by grace divine he trampled
  Out each lustful creeping sin,

And stood forth a God-devoted
  Victor o'er the carnal man,
To build up for lofty uses
  A new life with godly plan.

Then his soul went outward, reading
　　The strange omens of the time,
When to be a king meant licence
　　To give holy names to crime;

When a man who dared to stand
　　Erect, uncowed, before a king,
With old law and right behind him,
　　Was the first to feel the sting

Of the waspish vengeful weakling
　　Who, when propped up on a throne,
Deemed all power in earth and heaven
　　Centred in his whim alone.

OLIVER had seen the Stuart
　　In his uncle's hall of state,
With big rolling eye, and dribbling
　　Mouth, and loosely-shambling gait;

Mighty man to round a sentence
　　That might serve a schoolman's need,

Weak to know what, how, or whither,
　　When the hour called for a deed.

Bridled long by kilted chieftains,
　　Now, like bird with uncaged wing,
On the ample stage of England
　　James would grandly play the king.

Like a Cæsar he would king it;
　　He would teach them to behave,
As a master flogs a schoolboy,
　　As an owner whips a slave.

He would be a god, and god it
　　Bravely, bravely like the Pope;
And whose tongue denied his godship,
　　His stiff neck should know the rope.

Fool! a fresh young blood was pulsing
　　In the people; and a school
Of stout-hearted God-taught teachers
　　Kicked against all despot rule.

People now with eyes untutored
 Freely read the Word of Grace,
Seeing God, as Moses saw Him
 On the mountain, face to face.

Not from Pope or priest or patriarch
 Tamely now they took command ;
But true brother common-blooded
 Walked with brother hand in hand,

Children of no earthly father ;
 Kings might stamp for right the wrong,
But with God's still voice within him
 Each man for himself was strong.

This he knew not, the unkingliest
 King that ever fed on pride,
Deeming with fine-woven speeches
 To drive back the ocean's tide :

And so died ; but not with him
 Died the whim that fooled his brain :

In the son, more finely moulded,
  All the father lives again ;

All the lust to king it rarely,
  Like a Cæsar, like a god,
Like a Jove that all might tremble
  At the shadow of his nod ;

All the joy to shine supremely
  Like a sun on central throne,
Whence all fine vivific virtue
  Flows in strength from him alone ;

All the dear conceit of kingship
  To invest his royal home
With the purple pomp of priesthood,
  With the sacred pride of Rome.

Charles, and Laud, and haughty Strafford,
  They have sworn, all undismayed,
Or by daring, or cajoling,
  They will rule, and ask no aid

From the niggard cross-grained people,
   Looking with a jealous frown
On the gold which gilds the mitre,
   On the gems that star the crown.

But not reasoned thus the people;
   Norman blood and Saxon bone,
They had minds, and they had muscle,
   They had hearts they called their own.

They had souls to God devoted,
   Leal to law, and sworn to right;
For the chartered use of England
   They will stand and they will fight.

In the North a storm was brewing:
   In Dunedin, in Dunbar,
From the bristling breasts of Scotsmen
   Came the harsh alarm of war.

O'er the grave-stones of their fathers
   Holy hands were lifted high,

Solemn oaths by peer and peasant,
  Sworn in God's all-seeing eye,

Nevermore, with open Bibles
  And sharp swords to serve their need,
Shall an English priest for Scotsmen
  Clip the pattern of their creed.

Not in courtly phrase, or rubric
  Framed to please a pedant's whim,
But as free as bird in greenwood
  They will pour the heart-felt hymn.

They will preach in plain presentment
  From a freeman's manly breast,
Even as Paul, *sans* cope, *sans* surplice,
  Freely gospelled all the West.

They will pray at no dictation
  To compel unfelt desires,
Bend the knee at no man's bidding,
  As a puppet owns the wires.

And in England king and people,
  Pulling each his diverse way,
Left the State ship in the middle
  Leaking more from day to day.

Thrice five years of fretful talking
  Brought no fruit but bitter strife,
More and more the knots were tangled
  That called loudly for the knife.

And the knife began its mission
  With much din, now here now there,
Blindly plunging, grandly dashing,
  Blood and blunders everywhere,

Half right, half wrong. Not all who struck
  The nail for right, would drive it in,
Weak of purpose, slow to finish
  What they hasted to begin.

Dukes and earls, half-hearted weaklings,
  Fearing much the monarch's pride,

Fearing more the people's strong arm
　When they cast all fear aside !

Courtly men will deal no blows
　To make a strong-willed despot pause ;
When the people fight, a captain
　From the people wins their cause.

CROMWELL came ; nor came alone,
　But with him, to do or die,
Honest men of his own choosing,
　Fighting in the master's eye.

Not gay youths with knightly titles,
　Riding, dancing, gambling, swearing,
Waving plumes, and prancing horses,
　With light-hearted dash of daring ;

Such were good to fight for courtly
　Ladies' smile and grace of kings ;
But with firm persistent purpose,
　Through the stress and strain of things,

For the truth they loved to risk all,
  Sinking low or mounting high,
Doing daily prayerful duty,
  As in God's all-seeing eye;

For such feats of high-souled manhood,
  Where God's supreme law presides,
Other tools must shape his action,
  Hearts of steel, and iron sides.

Men in yeomen's craft well trained
  To split the rock and cleave the sod;
Hands made strong by sweatful labour,
  Hearts made strong by faith in God.

Men in hour of sharpest strain,
  Who, mildly strong and sternly calm,
Braced their thought with memoried Scripture,
  Cheered their heart with chaunted psalm.

"Gentlemen are good," quoth CROMWELL,
  "Softly bred, and smoothly dressed;

But a man, to win a battle,
  Must bear victory in his breast ;

" Plainly fed and russet-coated,
  And with hands inured to toil,
And a cause he joys to fight for,
  Let Dame Fortune frown or smile.

" Princes love to lead great armies ;
  But when God has work to do,
Or for gospel or for battle,
  He makes strong a chosen few."

Other men might loosely waver ;
  But when CROMWELL eyed the foe,
Or at Marston or at Naseby,
  Like Jove's bolt came down the blow.

Other men might dash and rattle ;
  But with thoughtful plan prepared,
In the hour of quick decision
  CROMWELL was the man who dared.

Charles was vanquished : like a hunted
    Fox from shift to shift he flew ;
When a fair-faced lie might fail him,
    Ever spinning something new.

Ever sowing seeds of faction,
    Never to his promise true ;
Throwing yeast into the ferment
    Where dissension rankly grew.

But not CROMWELL might be juggled
    By fair speech or slippery word ;
Shifty king, and friends half-hearted,
    Both should know he bore the sword.

Time is none for talking, tinkering,
    When storms rage and seas o'erwhelm ;
Let him die whose faithless purpose
    Brought confusion on the realm.

King or cobbler born, what matter,
    With a crown or with a hat ;

Who would crush his people's freedom,
    Let the false king die for that!

And they tried him for a traitor;
    And they brought him forth to die
At Whitehall upon a scaffold,
    In the people's wondering eye.

Who shall rule a headless nation?
    Charles had left a son, a youth,
Like himself a shuffling schemer,
    Foe to goodness and to truth.

Him the Scots, unwisely loyal,
    Crowned with kingly grace at Scone,
Unprophetic of the falsehood
    Bred in every Stuart's bone.

Not so CROMWELL—he who never
    Helped a serpent's brood to sting,
Trained too well to know the Devil's
    Game played with the name of king.

At Dunbar he took his station;
  There with scanted strength stood he,
Where the old grey castle looks forth
  Grimly on the old grey sea.

Westward to the hills he turns
  His watchful glance both quick and sure,
And there the Scots he saw in thousands
  Marshalled on the old grey moor.

Meagre hope was there for CROMWELL;
  They might hedge him round and round,
From their chosen post of vantage
  On the high and heathy ground.

Leslie was a stout old soldier,
  Wary as a Scot may be,
And he saw sure prey in CROMWELL,
  With his back beside the sea.

But strange things will chance; and Leslie,
  To his vantage-ground untrue,

Down the hill with forward rashness
　　Strangely came to CROMWELL'S view.

" Pounce upon them ! on, brave boys !
　　On through mist and moony gleam ;
On ! the Lord of hosts is with us ;
　　On ! yon sun's first rising beam

" Shines on victory ! pounce upon them !
　　By my faith, they run, they run !
God hath scattered them before us
　　As the mist flies from the sun !"

On he rushes like a torrent ;
　　Back they flee in blank amaze ;
On he rolls with volleyed thunder,
　　On with swelling hymns of praise.

They are routed.　Stout old Scotland
　　Stands a public fool confessed,
When she took a wounded adder
　　Blindly to her kindly breast.

L

But where is Charles?   With fond assurance
    He hath risked to front his foes
'Mid fair England's wooded greenery,
    Where the Severn gently flows.

Vainly; for, with pace of thunder,
    Sleepless CROMWELL follows there,
And like houseless wild beast drives him,
    Hunted hot from lair to lair,

Till he changed high-hearted England
    For a land beyond the seas,
Where kings, by fretful parties' goad
    Unvexed, might eat and drink at ease.

Now the stage is cleared from kings;
    But Parliaments in high debate
Nurse dissent, and breed confusion
    With their never-ending prate.

CROMWELL hath no craft of talking,
    Loves to go the shortest road;

Right into the hall of council,
 As a soldier strides, he strode.

"Take away that bauble—shadows
 Are ye of what once ye were !
England hath no need of shadows ;
 I am CROMWELL : I am here,

" Weighted with no trifling business :
 This poor farce will never do ;
Better men must fill your places :
 Hence ! the Lord hath done with you !"

And they went as wanton schoolboys,
 When the master shows his rod,
Or as idols from the presence
 Vanish of the rightful God.

He hath conquered. Clad in plain grey
 Hose, and worsted stockings grey,
And a hat without a hat-band,
 He is England's king to-day.

No more shaking now and shuffling,
   No more swaying to and fro ;
Now the strong man rules, all England
   Feels, and Europe soon shall know.

Now no more to haughty Spaniards
   Britons basely bow the head,
No more paid by Frankish bounty
   Hireling troops are basely fed.

No more hordes of plundering pirates
   Fill our well-stored ports with fears,
Turk and Tuscan strike their colours
   Where the flag of Blake appears.

At the mighty word of CROMWELL
   Popes are dumb, and curses cease ;
And in Alpine valleys godly
   Peasants sing their psalms in peace.

England's hand is felt in Europe
   Now, as in the good old time

Of Plantagenets in their glory,
　Of the Tudors in their prime.

But no man is blest in all things :
　Feared at Paris, feared in Rome,
Hot contention grew around him,
　With unkindly thoughts at home.

He had saved them from the despot,
　He had helped them in their need,
And with best heart's blood of England
　Watered freedom's precious seed.

But the tumult and the grating
　Jar of jealous power with power,
Not even his strong will might charm it
　To sweet music in an hour.

And he died with work unfinished ;
　But, with life's flood ebbing low,
" I have sown good seed," he said,
　" And God will know to make it grow."

WASHINGTON.

I will sing the grand New World,
  I will sing God's elect man,
Dowered with strength divine to found it
  On a new high-fortuned plan.

Meagre souls there be who fancy
  God as meagre as themselves,
That His tale of things was ended
  With the books upon their shelves !

With the record of their glories,
  Battles, blunders, brawls and blood,
When high-vaulting Whigs and Tories
  Clutched the stars, or kissed the mud !

Foolish ! sooner might a starveling,
  Begging pence from door to door,
Know what millions mean, when counted
  In a rich man's golden store,

Than the self-spun speculation
  Of the mole-eyed minion man,
Tell the bearings of the broad-winged
  Stretch of God's far-sweeping plan !

Poets dream, and scheming sages
  Pile Utopias all their own ;
But the greatest of all dreamers
  Is a fool upon a throne.

James the Scot was king and coward,
  Pedant, fool, and fox to boot,
With a brain that fondled fancies,
  And a deft tongue for dispute.

Born was he in fretful Albyn
  Where the prickly thistle grows,

Which he grasped with bleeding fingers :
Now he dwells in soft repose,

Dwells in majesty of Whitehall,
Where the Tudors had their will ;
Here the Scot shall heir their fortunes
With a braver mission still.

He will king it grandly, grandly,
Like crowned heads beyond the sea,
From his ring of stiff-souled barons,
From his rude-mouthed preachers, free.

Preachers, curs ! an unwhipt nation,
Barking in their master's face,
Who should wear their gilded collars
At his feet with crouching grace,

Bring them hither ! He hath seen them,
He hath heard them for his sport,
With brave show of Latin learning,
From his throne in Hampton Court.

He hath heard their humble craving,
  Loyal suit for mild release
From harsh Tudor-laws that hindered
  Pious souls to pray in peace.

Only as a priest might drill them,
  Or a king with penal rod,
Might they pour the heavy burden
  Of their sins before their God.

But the good and godly people
  Read God's holy book with awe,
And they read no praise of bishops
  There, or kings above the law.

Cæsar's things they gave to Cæsar,
  Things of God they gave to God;
But to stint free breath in prayer
  To bishop's mace and monarch's rod,

God denies. But James took counsel
  Blindly with his blinded mind :

" Let them go !—we may not harbour
    Vermin of this saucy kind !

" Let them wander far from England,
    There to hug their private notion,
To the land of dykes and ditches,
    To wide wastes beyond the ocean !

" Kings were useless might each unlearned
    Bible-speller forge a creed ;
Kings bear rule from God's fair garden
    Forth to pluck the baneful weed ! "

Thus he spake.   The godly people
    From crowned folly wisely fled
To the land of dykes and ditches,
    Where young Freedom reared her head ;

Nor there tarried long.   More faithful
    To their king than he to them,
They would draw their sapful virtue
    Still from England's lusty stem.

From the land of dykes and ditches,
  Down the sluggish Maas they creep,
On to Plymouth, where Old England
  Stout her naval watch doth keep.

Thence with hearts to God devoted,
  And with souls from slavery free,
They have sailed, the godly people,
  Westward, westward o'er the sea.

Through the heaving high-towered billows
  Storms that rage with savage glee,
With split masts and creaking timbers,
  To a land where thought is free.

There to found a brave New England,
  Mighty tree from little seed,
Where no sophist-king might dare
  To twist a text, or carve a creed.

They have landed in the shallows
  'Neath thy sheltering wing, Cape Cod ;

There they knee the sand in thankful
  Worship to their Saviour God.

They have looked about with wonder
  On the strange new-customed strand,
Trees on trees in plumy grandeur
  Waving fragrance from the land.

They have looked upon the broad bay
  Where huge whales are spouting high,
On the creeks where ducks and wild geese
  Sport, all gleefully and shy.

They have sent their best and bravest,
  Standish fearles and adroit,
To explore the riskful traces
  Of the red-skinned Massasoit.

They have seen the black-haired nation
  Plumed and feathered like a fan,
Wild, uncouth, uncomely people,
  Like the roving gipsy clan !

And they made truce with the people,
  Faithful vows that they should be
Free from harm from sons of England,
  Born with birthright to be free !

And they built their town beside them,
  Nicely measured ; row on row
Each man built his rough-hewn dwelling,
  That the work might bravely grow.

And they built a church and schoolhouse
  With fair front and goodly show,
That the town, with God's good blessing
  On the work, might chastely grow.

And it grew ; but slowly, slowly,
  As sweet flowers 'neath frosty dew ;
Cold and sickness and starvation
  Made them dwindle to a few ;

Few but faithful ; though with bleeding
  Foot the unschooled soil they trod,

Still they plied their earth-subduing
  Task, and praised their Saviour God.

And they piled a brave new Plymouth,
  Founded by the salt sea-foam,
On a rock like that Tarpeian ridge
  That cradled mighty Rome!

Nor alone on Nausite waters,
  Where the grampus spouts and rolls
For a grand new world of freemen
  God prepared His ransomed souls.

Southward too, beyond the Hudson,
  Where Potómac pours his flood
Grew to manly firm consistence
  English life from English blood.

There from civil feud and faction,
  Hatred, jealousy, and strife,

Noble men of pith and prudence
  Sought and found a peaceful life ;

Life like Adam's in the garden,
  Digging, delving, planting, sowing,
Like the stout old Cincinnati,
  When the pride of Rome was growing.

There in use of hardy nurture,
  From wise father wiser son,
To the strength of stately manhood
  Grew the noble WASHINGTON.

God had shaped him for a leader :
  With his playmates in the school
GEORGE was mild and GEORGE was modest,
  But they felt that he must rule.

First was he in every youthful
  Sport ; supreme in mimic wars,
Racing, leaping, wrestling, swimming,
  Pitching quoits and tossing bars.

If a horse was fierce and furious,
    With kick and start and caracole,
Only GEORGE could hold the rider's seat
    With kingly firm control.

Thoughtful too; not hot and heady,
    But with measured grace and slow;
Where his cool eye made the survey,
    There he launched the well-poised blow.

Not a man of random plunges,
    Dash, and dart, and snatch was he;
But he stood, as stands a pilot
    In the many-tossing sea,

Master of himself; the planets,
    In their measured going on,
Wheel not with a march more steady
    Than the soul of WASHINGTON.

With no wavering consecration
    Of the manliest thing in man,

He had gaged his life to duty
On a holy-purposed plan.

Trained in field-work, trained in camp-work,
Like his work, his mind was true;
Line by line, like wise besieger,
To his aim he nearer drew.

Times are ripening for his counsel,
For his strength, and for his daring;
West beyond the Alleghany,
Seeds of prickly strife are bearing

Bloody fruit. On the Ohio,
With huge lust of large command,
France with vulture-wings was hovering
O'er Virginia's happy land,

Where the Shenandoah, daughter
Of the stars, with fruitful flood
Grandly rolling, softly swirling,
Waters many a pine-clad rood.

With delayful and unskilful
    Counsel England saw the Franks,
In the Northland and the Westland
    Pile their forts in bristling ranks;

Saw, and sent a boastful captain,
    In the strange wild warfare rude,
With sharp word and stroke to humble
    Haughty Gaul's defiant mood.

Vainly; wilful-counselled Braddock,
    With proud front and haughty nose,
Fell, as evermore the braggart
    Falls who lightly holds his foes.

Not so WASHINGTON, who followed
    Where the beaten boaster fell;
Wise and wary, in wild warfare
    At Potomac practised well.

Well he knew the red-skinned nations,
    Ever threatful, never sure,

Quick to start from unseen covert,
  Like the wild bird on the moor;

Skulking now in leafy ambush,
  Rattling now like stony hail,
Weak to stand in serried phalanx,
  Where the marshalled lines prevail.

He their flooded streams had breasted,
  Slept in rain and camped in snow,
With an eagle eye had followed
  Where a hunter's foot might go.

With quick start of fiery venture,
  Like the spreading of a flame,
To the fork of mighty waters
  In Ohio's vale he came;

To the strong fort where the Frenchman,
  Sweeping all the Western plain
From the Lakes down Mississippi,
  Claimed the haughty right to reign.

And the British flag he planted
    On the steep brow of Du Quesne,
At the forking of the waters,
    Whence the Frenchmen vexed the plain.

And they fled as flee the pigeons,
    When the hawk swoops down amain,
From the forking of the waters
    Nevermore to vex the plain ;

Never from that height to flourish
    Trenchant blade and supple wit,
New baptised for England's glory
    With the noble name of PITT !

———

Years rolled on.   In lusty boyhood,
    With brave front and shining face,
From Virginia to St Lawrence
    Grew the grand New World apace.

But the mother of the brave boy,
    Far with blindly groping hands
Deemed the boy was still a baby,
    Needful of her swaddling-bands.

And she sent unskilful nurses
    'Cross the wide Atlantic flood,
Some to spur the baby's pulses,
    Some to suck the baby's blood.

Motley nurses, titled nurses,
    Soldiers, courtiers, lords, and earls,
Talking much of needful nursing,
    Dreaming much of gold and pearls.

But the boy was rough and rampant,
    Baby would be hight no more,
He would use his legs at pleasure,
    Keep the key of his own store.

Lusty babes disown the mother's
    Tearful cares and fingering hands;

Sturdy boys fling back the father's
  Word that cramps while it commands.

So the quarrel grew.   In London,
  Ignorance from haughty breast
Vowed a vow of sharp correction
  To the baby in the West.

But the baby, like Alcmena's
  Jove-born son, when Greece began,
Snapt his bands, and stood erect
  With face of boy and soul of man.

Men of Plymouth and of Boston,
  Had they fled beyond the waves
Only for a change of masters,
  With the unchanged name of slaves?

Had the evil-counselled Stuarts
  Bled and fled and fought in vain,
And shall dull-brained Hanoverians
  Tempt the despot's game again?

No! Stout Saxon-blooded yeomen
   Never kissed a tyrant's rod;
They too had their Magna Charta
   From wise William and from God.

They would pay their own State-servants,
   Measured work for measured fee;
They would drink, untaxed, unrated,
   Their own wine and their own tea.

Free is none who owns a master
   On far throne beyond the sea;
Only those who use a home-bred
   Ruler, know that they are free.

Thus outspake brave Boston's freemen,
   And with one stroke snapt their gyves;
But the pig-brained Hanoverian
   Still would stir the fire with knives.

With wise prophet's voice of warning,
   Burke their courtly ears assailed;

But the brainless and the boastful
    In the strife of words prevailed ;

Words that meant sharp swords. To Boston's
    Island-fretted ample bay
England sent her hireling Hessians,
    And her ships in brave array,

There to stamp out holy Freedom,
    And to block Time's forward way,
And to bind the arms of labour
    'Neath a wilful despot's sway.

And she did so—for a twelvemonth
    And a day. The storm was brewing,
Doomed to whelm the rash offender,
    When God's hour was ripe for doing.

Short-lived was her hour of triumph,
    Harsh command and lawless will ;
Roaring cannon, blazing rafters,
    Tumbling forts at Bunker Hill,

Spurred the breath they could not stifle ;
  Prick a lion, and he stands
Ten times lion, like a Titan
  Flailing with a hundred hands.

From the South a cry resounded,
  Manful pulse to pulse replied,
Nevermore to free-born brother
  Be a brother's help denied !

And they made a league together,
  And they sent their noblest son,
Tried in fight and tried in counsel,
  Faithful-hearted WASHINGTON,

From his pleasant home at Vernon,
  With fair prospect far and wide,
With rich stretch of wealthy culture,
  With its amply-flowing tide.

Him they made their elect-captain,
  Him they missioned *sans* delay,

With free-mustered bands to Boston's
  Island-fretted ample bay.

There he watched, and there he waited,
  With a firm and faithful caring,
Shaping cosmos from the chaos,
  Till the hour was ripe for daring.

Then with swift assault unfearing,
  Scaled a ridge above the bay,
And with iron hail tremendous,
  Sent in startled disarray

Howe and Percy, and the boastful
  Troop that crossed the Western waves,
With an arm of sharp compulsion
  To teach freemen to be slaves.

Outward, Eastward, swiftly, swiftly,
  Swiftlier than they came, they fled,
Nevermore in face of Boston's
  Free-sworn front to lift their head!

War has many chances ; not one
   Swallow makes the spring, one bud
Not the summer. Born in sorrow
   Sharply, and baptised in blood,

Grows the babe that makes the people ;
   Not one victory for the right
Could prevail to lop the crest
   Of England, ever stiff in fight.

Howe was not a name to marry
   With defeat and blank dismay ;
Southward he would steer his warships,
   With fresh hope and larger sway.

Where the strong son of the Highlands,
   Hudson, rolls his ample flood,
He would stamp out the untutored
   Growth of freedom in the bud.

In New York's fair water-belted,
   Island-forted, busy mart,

He would rise from short prostration,
  Strong to play the conqueror's part.

He would prove here that Old England,
  Or with fair or adverse breeze,
In Pacific or Atlantic,
  Ever knows to rule the seas.

And he did it. O'er Manhattan's
  Long-drawn isle his might prevailed,
And at peaceful Philadelphia
  Him the meek-souled Quakers hailed.

He hath wiped the blot of Boston
  From his scutcheon. Delaware
And wide Hudson roll their floods,
  To teach the West that Howe is there.

There indeed; but towns and rivers
  Which proud England called her own,
Never cast a shade of shrinking
  O'er the heart of WASHINGTON.

He had sworn to stand for freedom,
   If not safely here, then there;
Hearts were brave, and men had mettle,
   Westward of the Delaware.

Doubting oft, despairing never,
   With a starved and shoeless host;
Firm in faith and wise in daring,
   While he breathed all was not lost.

Never is the greatness greater
   Than when dangers grimly swell,
Like a tide of mighty billows
   Rushing, racing, fierce and fell.

Never is the bright hope brighter
   In a God-devoted soul,
Than when clouds in massy volume
   Blot the sky and blind the pole.

As a tiger in the jungle
   Patient waits day after day,

Till the moment comes, then pounces
    Sudden on his 'scapeless prey ;

So Virginia's elect captain,
    Wise to wait nor slow to dare,
With his band of true-sworn freemen
    Eastward crossed the Delaware.

"Now, brave boys, be ready, ready,
    Use the chance the moment brings;
When their strength is loosely scattered,
    Now's the time to clip their wings !

"'Tis the day of Merry Christmas ;
    Through the river's chilly flow,
Through the snowdrift and the ice-blocks,
    March we now against the foe,

"Merrily, merrily ! Hireling Hessians,
    Smoking, bousing, soon shall know
How to hold a bloody Christmas
    When they face a patriot foe !"

So said, so done.   The towers of Trenton
   Nod submission to his word ;
North from Trenton, on to Princeton,
   All New Jersey's heart is stirred ;

And the proud invading foeman
   Shorn of hope, of glory bare,
And with wings well pruned, retreated
   From the banks of Delaware.

Nor alone in reborn Jersey ;
   Freedom grew where WASHINGTON
Made the country and the river
   Breathe a spirit all his own.

In the North at Saratoga,
   Where the healthful water flows,
Boastful Burgoyne caught, in 'scapeless
   Trap by many-circling foes,

Piled his arms in meek surrender ;
   And through all the banded States

Rose with firmer pulse the patriots'
    Hope to greet the beckoning Fates.

Turn we now to Carolina,
    On a softlier-nurtured folk,
Where Cornwallis and stout Hastings
    Laid the sharply-galling yoke

For a season; but not longer;
    Though they strewed the plains with death,
Ever from the free-souled Northland
    Came the fresh reviving breath;

From the Northland, where the elect
    Captain, hoping against hope,
Watched and waited for the moment
    When his purpose might have scope.

And he found a friend to aid him
    In the pressure of the hour,
France, that ever looked with jealous
    Eye on England's branching power;

France he won to do his bidding,
  That she sent in pennoned pride
Lines of bravely mounted war-ships
  O'er the broad Atlantic tide,

With young Freedom to hold counsel,
  And with common soul conspire,
How for England's castigation,
  Saxon strength and Celtic fire

Might be banded.   From the Hudson
  Swift to move, and strong to dare,
To his own Virginian waters
  Came the elect captain, there

With his presence to turn England's
  Forward marches to retreat,
And strike the gyves through all the Southland
  From young Freedom's sacred feet.

In a nook by long-drawn waters
  Fenced around, as in a net,

How can brave Cornwallis slip
From WASHINGTON and Lafayette?

Like a baited beast in York Town,
With stout English heart he stands,
With redoubts and batteries many,
Restless raised by sleepless hands.

Vainly; as storm-clouds come creeping
Slowly, darkly from the West,
So the circling death-lines nearer
Came and nearer to his breast.

For three days and four the fatal
Fire-mouths bellowed round the town;
Rafters blazed, and towers of triple-
Forted strength came crashing down.

All the day was streaked with blackness,
Blotting beauty from the air;
All the night was bright with meteors,
Streaming with a deadly glare.

Nearer still and ever nearer
 Came the stern avoidless lines,
Brighter still and still more bright
 The flaring belt of terror shines.

Then, as storm-nursed waves Atlantic
 Overlash the steep rock's crown,
So with fearless sweep the scalers
 Clomb the walls and held the town.

Ever in the van of danger,
 Cool and firm stood WASHINGTON,
Careless where a shot might wander,
 If the work was bravely done.

Where he stood in an embrasure,
 Open to a deathful shot,
One with friendly fear besought him
 Back to step to safer spot.

"Seek your safety," said the Captain,
 "If it like you ; I will not.

I will stand where honour calls me,
 Though red Death may mark the spot."

Thus he stood and thus he conquered,
 With the strength that arms the free,
Till the stout heart of Cornwallis,
 Vexed by land and vexed by sea,

Bowed his head in meek surrender,
 And, from dreams of victory free,
Found a second Saratoga
 Where York river seeks the sea.

Little now remained for Freedom's
 Sons to do; the work was done
By the patient, long-enduring,
 Steadfast faith of WASHINGTON.

There was talking much in London,
 Much in Paris; but all knew
Freedom's cause was safe, while freemen
 To their chief's high will were true.

Parleys and negotiations
  Had their hour ; with wisdom late,
Fretful king and fuming courtier
  Signed the deed that sealed their fate.

On the banks of Hudson river,
  When the peace-sworn foe was gone,
In New York, at Whitehall ferry,
  Stood the noble WASHINGTON.

Not alone : in brothered sadness
  Round him stood his comrades brave,
Who for eight long years of hardship,
  Strong to suffer and to save,

Strove with him, and served him gladly,
  As an angel serveth God,
Drawing strength from his sereneness,
  Reaping victory from his nod.

And he spoke as one that could not,
  Broken words, and slow to come ;

Shallow grief delights in phrases,
  Grief that holds the heart is dumb.

"Brim this glass," he said, "brave brothers,
  Here in wine, and here in tears—
Wine for the great joy that crowned us,
  Tears for wounds that gashed the years.

"God be with you in your peaceful
  Harvest, as He stood by you
When you sowed the seed of honour,
  Watered with the bloody dew!"

And they came with head low drooping,
  Each man, and with eyes all dim,
This last once to feel a brother's
  Love in kindly grasp from him.

Not a word was spoken; silent
  They; and silent he moved on,
Where a modest barge was waiting
  For the noble WASHINGTON.

And with homeward heart he hied him
   To the town of good Queen Anne,
Where the People's congress waited
   To receive their Saviour-man.

And he came and stood before them,
   As a modest servant stands,
And with few plain words he gave
   His missioned power into their hands.

And they gave with solemn plainness
   All the thanks that words could give ;
And he went to sweet Mount Vernon,
   As a plain man lives to live.

Some had been once that would make him
   King, that he might grandly reign
O'er them like a Roman Cæsar ;
   But with high-souled proud disdain

Back he flung the base suggestion ;
   For his country he had fought,

He had gained his country's freedom,
    That was all he wished or sought.

Not for gold, and not for glory,
    He the thorny path had trod,
But in name of sacred duty
    To his country and his God.

So he then ; and now, as only
    Lofty self-poised souls can do,
All the public pomp behind him
    Like a cumbrous coat he threw.

Even as Roman Cincinnatus,
    In the days when Rome was wise,
He would watch his old paternal
    Acres with paternal eyes.

And he lived in homely sweetness,
    Deeming pride the worst of sinning ;
Planting, pruning, delving, draining,
    From the soil its riches winning.

Ever on the work before him
  Fixed with kindly-searching eyes,
Great in small things as in greatest,
  And in daily service wise.

Till they brought him from his covert,
  To their march of storied fame,
To give grace and goodly omen
  With the blazon of his name.

NELSON AND WELLINGTON.

I.

I WILL sing of England's glory,
　　Daring dash, and cool command,
When her brave high-hearted captains
　　Rode the sea and ruled the land;

When amid the strife of nations,
　　Wise by war to purchase peace,
Her firm hand compelled the plundering
　　Lust of lawless France to cease,

France the beacon of the nations;
　　France, aflame with wrath—and why?

Lords with no wise craft of lordship,
  Kings unkingly make reply.

Loveless laws that knew no poor man,
  Loveless lords that knew no shame,
When they starved the sweatful ploughman,
  When they fed the guarded game.

Loveless kings that knew no measure
  When their pride was mounted high,
Knew no manhood when well-baited
  Hooks seduced the sensual eye.

Insolence and lust and riot
  Of the few in pampered state,
With the lean-eyed many grimly
  Pining at the palace gate.

Creed that brooked no talk with reason,
  Churches hollow, priests unwise
Mumbling spells in name of Jesus,
  To give saintly gloss to lies.

Sin was rank in court and castle,
   Earth was sick; the hour was nigh
When the sure slow-footed Fury
   Marched with vengeance from the sky;

When the smothered grudge of ages
   From dark womb of discontent
Burst in flames of blood-red portent
   On the lowering firmament.

Woe to them that in their dreaming
   Think that God with them may sleep!
Through their sleeping He is raising
   Earthquakes from the fiery deep;

Through their sleep their thrones are rocking,
   Towers of pride are falling low,
And they start up from their slumbers
   To behold a march of woe!

Blood-red banners, flags of terror,
   Surging tumult, grim affright,

Tocsin from a hundred churches
Sounding through the startled night;

Thick as wasps with stings well pointed,
Glaring eyes, hands high to strike,
Dusty doublets red with murder,
Heads of traitors on a pike.

Frantic women, screaming children,
Raving Mænads drunk with hate,
Through the fevered streets parading
In tempestuous foaming state.

Vengeance raging, Fury blazing,
Madness marching in the van;
All the tiger, all the demon,
Leaping from the depths of man.

Woe to them that through the ages
Sleep, when watchmen should have eyes!
They shall wake when red-eyed Terror
Floods the earth and blots the skies.

Terror, terror, ghastly terror,
  Now the order of the day;
Every shape and sign of terror
  Stalking forth in red display.

Terror now with pace of thunder,
  Spectre dance, and ghostly skipping,
Sightless eyes all blind with weeping,
  Sundered heads all gory dripping;

Heads of kings that knew no sinning,
  Heads of queens that knew no fear,
Heads of hero-hearted maidens,
  Trundled on a butcher's bier!

As the grass before the mower
  Falls in swathes upon the green,
So fall fairest heads and noblest
  'Neath the wide-jawed guillotine!

Guillotining, fusilading,
  One by one is far too slow;

Shoot them, crush them, overwhelm them
  In one thunder-peal of woe !

Fusilading and noyading !
  In an ark with no salvation
Huddled, they are swamped with deluge
  From the mad wrath of the nation.

Lo ! they mingle glee with madness :
  Drunk with rancour to the brim,
They have made a painted harlot
  Goddess of their godless whim ;

All that charmed the chaste-souled reason,
  Order, beauty, trampled low,
Liberty with beastly licence,
  All the piety they know.

Such a revel of the Furies,
  Such red train of ghastly mirth,
God hath sent from depths demoniac
  To chastise the sons of earth.

Learn, ye kings! be wise, ye peoples!
   Let not lusty sin grow strong;
Weeds that grow to poison-blossoms
   Should be plucked when they are young.

II.

The fit is o'er, the fever fit
   Of blind rage and red confusion—
The five years' fever of wild France,
   'Clept by mortals Revolution.

Who hath banned it? A young soldier.
   He, in force a firm believer,
With a weighty whiff of grape-shot
   Swiftly banned the raging fever.

Sobered now, proud France looks round her;
   And, behold! on sounding wings,
All the banded monarchs gathered
   To avenge her slight of kings.

Prince and princeling on the Rhineland,
   Purse-proud merchants on the sea,
All that dare to scowl on freedom
   Now shall know that France is free !

France is free ; and, like Alcides
   When he snapt his baby-bands,
She decrees sharp war on tyrants,
   East and west, in slavish lands.

She will free the peoples ; chiefly
   Free herself, to hold in awe
All the cowering, crouching millions,
   When her sword hath shaped the law.

She hath sent that strong-brained youngling,
   With keen glance, and lips compressed,
And an ocean of far-reaching
   Deep devisings in his breast,

To the land where Pope and Kaiser
   Long had held our souls in thrall,

o

There to preach the red Evangel,
   Forged in France for great and small.

As an eagle on the quarry,
   Swiftly pounced that wondrous boy,
Playing with a Titan foeman
   As a child plays with a toy.

Light, and with no lumbering baggage
   Groaning o'er the stony path,
His own herald ; as when thunder
   Bursts with unexpected wrath,

He hath turned the Alps the Punic
   Captain crossed with sweatful pains,
And his eye prophetic ranges
   O'er wide wealth of green domains.

And he scans their crescent barrier
   Crowned with peaks of shining snow,
And his proud heart beats exultant
   As his fancy doomed the foe.

Vainly Alps shall shield the Austrian,
  Vainly shield the hireling Swiss,
When old lordship's frost-work melteth
  At young Freedom's fiery kiss.

So said, so done.   Small time for breathing
  In Turin's well-watered seat
He allows ; at half-way stations
  Whoso tarries courts defeat.

Austrians will be doubting, dreaming,
  Germans heavy, dull, and slow,
While he plants his flag three-coloured
  On the north bank of the Po.

Lo ! and at the bridge of Lodi,
  Where their legions block the tide,
He o'erleaps the many-throated
  Jaws of death, and stands in pride

On the road to Milan.   Milan,
  With its many-statued fane,

Hails the wondrous boy, whose strong arm
　　Snaps the hated German chain.

On to Mantua, to Lonato,
　　By fair Garda's gustful water,
There to fine the stiff old Austrian,
　　Slow to learn, with double slaughter.

What will stop him?　Aulic councils
　　In Vienna?　Nevermore.
Swift as tiger in the jungle,
　　Through the rattle and the roar

Of the volleyed death, defying
　　Fate, he stands; and Fate, that knew
Him to strange high ends predestined,
　　Brought the gallant bravely through.

Adige and Tagliamento
　　Set no bounds to his career;
Save and Drave flow crisped with terror
　　When his thunder-pace is near.

At Vienna, at Vienna,
  Hearts are faint and eyes are dim ;
Be he god, or be he devil,
  They must purchase peace from him.

He hath caught the holy Roman
  Cæsar in a mountain trap ;
Sulky Venice with one weighty
  Word he blotteth from the map.

And the Pope, that once made largess
  Of whole kingdoms like a god,
See him now meek doom receiving
  From a belted stripling's nod.

Wondrous boy, the scourge of nations !
  Whither now with lordly whim
Shall he wend him ?   Not in Paris
  Is the fruit yet ripe for him.

He can wait.   And what if Europe
  Were too scant a reach for him ?

Conquering Alexanders ever
   Sought the golden East, to swim

On the top wave of dominion.
   Let the ferment work ; and, while
Time breeds blunders, crowned with glory,
   From the famous loam of Nile,

He will come, and from Euphrates
   And great Babel's fatted plain,
Where the Nimrods of the old time
   Taught the primal kings to reign.

Thus he dreamed ; and thirsting ever
   For new venture and new spoil,
And new harm to stout Old England,
   On he thunders to the Nile.

III.

And the Nile he holds ; but only
   For an hour.   His check is nigh.

He who sits in heaven shall laugh
When proud man would scale the sky.

When the golden-headed image
Loftiest looks, with insolence crowned,
Lo! a stone rough from the mountain
Smites it level with the ground.

In the sandy loam of Norfolk,
Where the farmer hath his joy,
Where the church bells ring at Barnham,
NELSON grew, a weakly boy.

Weak in body, strong in spirit,
Brave as bravest boy may be;
Never shrinking, ever climbing
To the top branch of the tree.

You might note him on the playground,
You might mark him in the school,
With an air of swift decision,
Born to venture and to rule.

If a nest were to be plundered,
  Or a pear-tree on the wall,
High, too high for vulgar riskers,
  NELSON dared at danger's call.

Nursed in hardship, not on softly-
  Cushioned couch of ease, grew he
But in use of sailors roughly,
  Where the Medway seeks the sea

Learning as the sailor learneth,
  In the sunshine, in the shower,
In the near and in the far land,
  Waiting wisely on the hour.

In the land where fog and snowdrift
  Nurse the walrus and the bear,
'Neath the bright green-glancing icebergs,
  Wooing danger, he was there.

In the land of swamps and serpents,
  Where pale fever taints the air

Deadly, where the trees drop poison,[1]
Death-defying, he was there.

Through the wear and tear of service,
   Strong, erect, alert he stood,
True to honour, sworn to duty,
   Great in every manful mood.

Great men wait for great occasions;
   Great occasions wait for them,
To put forth the hand of daring,
   And to pluck the diadem

From unworthy brows. For Freedom
   Not, but for free hand to rule,
France now swept the globe with legions
   Trained in rapine's lawless school.

Like a watchman on a watch-tower,
   From her white cliffs on the sea

[1] Hippomane Mancinella ; order Euphorbiaceæ.

Stout Old England saw the Frankish
   Fetters forged to bind the free ;

Nor might stand alone, unfriending,
   Safely cased in selfish joy,
When all human rights were trampled
   'Neath that strong remorseless boy

Marching on to empire.   Never,
   While her ships might plough the main,
Shall that fell respectless Titan
   Vex free souls with galling chain.

Far from Nile and from Euphrates,
   Scornful of inglorious ease,
England sends her sailor-hero
   East and west to sweep the seas ;

Where the Frenchman, like a tiger,
   Whets his tusk and plants his paw,
There to hoist the flag of England,
   Pledge of honour and of law.

To the land that bore the Titan,
　Through the mid-sea's stormy swell,
NELSON hied, and at his coming
　Every bristling fortress fell.

Bastia bowed her towering crescent
　To his strength, and heard him say,
"One stout son of England matches
　Three deft Frenchmen in the fray."

Stately Calvi would defy him
　With four bastions mounted high,
But in vain—whose heart grew greater
　With the greater danger nigh.

Bravely done ; and, if not bravely
　Blazed before the public eye,
Days are coming, surely, swiftly,
　When Gazettes will fear to lie.

At St Vincent, with the Jervis,
　Where he came the Spaniard quailed ;

English pith and English mettle
   O'er his proud display prevailed.

With a forward spring of venture
   Light from ship to ship leaps he,
Strong as thunder, deft and agile
   As a squirrel on a tree.

England now is full of praises;
   London town with loud acclaim,
Bristol with her merchant princes,
   Lauds the gallant seaman's name.

Every ballad-singer knows him;
   Crowded streets, with shrill delight,
Hear the Jervis and the NELSON
   Sounded through the rainy night.

Joy was theirs; but NELSON, eager,
   Like a hound that holds the scent,
O'er the blastful mid-sea's windings
   Chased the Gallic armament

Till he found it, where Canopus,
  With his boldly jutting horn,
Bounds the broad bay, where the westmost
  Reach of Nile is seaward borne.

There he found them close-embattled,
  Thirteen ships in dense array,
With a deadly front of terror
  Eastward breasting all the bay.

Terror was delight to NELSON ;
  On the quarter or the bow
Of each ship he doubled round them,
  Pouring ruin on the foe !

On the fight down fell the darkness,
  And they saw with strange amaze,
Of the proud French line, the proudest
  Skyward shooting in a blaze.

Off they fled, like startled night-birds ;
  From the ruin of the fray,

Only two of all the thirteen
   Scuttled home in dire deray.

Off they fled ; and drifting with them
   Fled the dazzling dream like smoke,
Nile to bind, and eastmost Ganges,
   'Neath the Frenchman's haughty yoke.

Through the mid-sea's ransomed waters
   NELSON steered with steady might,
Leaving that proud boy to flounder
   Back to France in fretful flight.

Alp and Apennine nod welcome ;
   Naples, from her sun-bright bay,
Comes with streamers and with music,
   And with festive fair display,

Him to greet, high-hearted hero,
   Who had cleared the waters blue
From the rapine and the ravage
   Of the regicidal crew.

And the swart-faced Lazzaroni,
  In the transport of their glee,
To their birds unbarred the cages,
  In their plumy circuit free ;

And the fairest dame in Naples,
  When she saw that hero-boy,
Fell upon his arms and kissed him
  In grand ecstasy of joy.

Malta next, and fair Valetta,
  Hailed the chief, and blest the day
That saved her Christ-devoted waters
  From the godless Frenchman's sway.

Whither next? No rest for NELSON.
  Foiled and flouted in the East,
Now in Borean seas the Frenchman
  Sows his hot fermenting yeast.

He hath cowed the stiff old Austria ;
  Russia, Denmark, and the Swede,

Crouching 'neath his costly friendship,
　Now shall serve the tyrant's need.

But not England tholed a barrier
　Planted on the Baltic shore,
And she sent her son, her NELSON,
　Through the Sound by Elsinore,

Up to queenly Copenhagen,
　Where the bristling batteries be,
There to make the pride of Denmark
　Know the Power that sweeps the sea.

And they knew it.　As a hunter
　Brings the antlered troop to bay,
So with circling belt of thunder
　He enclosed their proud array,

Till their subject flag they lowered,
　And made free each Baltic isle,
From the Gallic bondage ransomed
　By the hero of the Nile.

England now with hymns of triumph
    Hails her hero. For a while,
Worn with labour, crowned with glory,
    He shall rest on British soil.

'Mid the leafy shades of Merton,
    Where the fishful Wandle flows,
With the friends that dearly love him,
    He will woo the sweet repose.

Here, instead of crested billows,
    Greening grass shall cheer his sight,
Greening grass and yellow waving
    Corn in summer's kindly light.

He will cherish pigs and poultry,
    Clip the sheep, and tend the hay ;
In the parish church on Sunday
    With the poor man he will pray.

Happy NELSON ! full of human-
    Hearted loving joy was he,

P

To the peasant, or the sailor
　　Tossed upon the fretful sea.

And they loved him—how they loved him !
　　For they said, " Our gallant NEL
Holds a heart wherein a lion
　　Knows in kindly peace to dwell

With a lamb."　A sweet-souled mother
　　Not more gently tends her boy,
Than NELSON with all men, the meanest,
　　Shared the sorrow and the joy.

Love and Peace in leafy Merton
　　Grew for NELSON ; but not long.
When his scourge again was needed
　　To chastise a giant wrong,

Forth he leapt at call of duty,
　　Leapt and dashed without delay
Right into the jaws of danger,
　　Where his presence signed the way

To bright issues. The French Titan,
  With unsated lust for war,
Now hath yoked the haughty Spaniard
  To his proud imperial car ;

And he sent his masted army
  O'er the mid-sea's swelling tide,
Through the billowy broad Atlantic,
  To bring down stout England's pride.

NELSON knows ; and he will chase them
  Through rude waves and stormy roar ;
Malta now, and now Palermo,
  Knows him ; now swart Barbary's shore.

He will chase them to the Indies,
  West and East, o'er all the seas,
With an eye that knows no sleeping,
  With a heart that knows no ease,

Till he find them. He hath found them
  Where Trafalgar fronts the brine,

Fiery Frank and haughty Spaniard,
  In a four-decked double line.

He hath gone below and prayed,
  With an holy consecration
Yielding up his life to God
  In a glorious consummation.

He hath gone aloft, and, breasted
  With four stars of honour, stands
On the deck, with his brave captains
  Waiting their great chief's commands.

And he gave the high-souled watchword,
  Not for glory or for booty,
But this only, "ENGLAND LOOKETH
  THAT EACH MAN SHALL DO HIS DUTY."

Right into the foeman's centre
  With a double wedge they broke,
Collingwood with noble NELSON
  Leading on the hearts of oak.

Where hot death poured from the Spaniard's
    Huge four-tiered Leviathan,
Bright and fearless there stood NELSON,
    Light as Hermes, in the van ;

Light as Hermes, as Alcides
    Strong, and breathing valiant breath,
But not wisely with his four-starred
    Breast of honour courting death.

Him they marked, and from the foeman's
    Mizzen-top a whizzing ball
Shot the brave man through the shoulder,
    And he fell as bird doth fall

On the moor before the sportsman.
    On his face he fell, and cried
To his faithful comrade Hardy,
    "Hardy, now I die ; the tide

"Of disrupted life is rushing
    Through unlicensed chambers. I

Would not live, but let me hear
    The shout of victory rend the sky !

"How goes it, Hardy?"   "Well! ten ships
    Have struck, the rest will strike anon ;
Maimed and mauled, they drift asunder,
    All their front of bravery gone."

"Then I die.   My love be with you !
    I have lived and loved not long ;
But, thank God, I did my duty,
    And I leave my country strong."

IV.

NELSON died ; and England triumphed,
    Mistress of the briny tide ;
But no hint from Fate brought warning
    To Napoleon's high-blown pride.

Like the Babylonian boaster,
    His vain heart was lifted up,

And he drank intoxication
From the despot's giddy cup.

Like a god his will shall portion
Kingdoms here and kingdoms there,
Where a field is free to plunder,
There the robber claims his share.

Stiff old Austria cowered before him,
Russia quailed, and Prussia bled;
Now the hot high-hearted Spaniard
Writhed beneath his iron tread;

Writhed and raged and foamed, and madly
Spat out rancour like a well,
Sowed the peaceful homes with murder,
Turning sweet life to a hell.

But not he for hell or heaven
Cared: so long his crested pride
On the back of harassed Europe
With high-booted strength might ride.

Europe shall be French ; a greater
  Now than Cæsar knows to reign ;
All her streams from Rhine to Danube
  Flood for him the fruitful plain.

Only England will not vail
  The high top-gallant of her might ;
She for justice, law, and freedom
  Still hath fought, and still will fight.

Not at Nile or at Trafalgar
  Her high-destined task was done ;
The seed brave NELSON sowed shall rise
  To full-grown strength in WELLINGTON.

In the castled hold of Dangan,
  On the peep of rosy May,
There, when moody France was brewing
  Horrors for no distant day,

Oped his baby eyes on sunlight
   WELLINGTON, sent forth by God
To give freedom to the nations
   Bleeding 'neath a despot's rod.

Not he shot up like a comet,
   Making every gaper stare,
But through sober scheme of schooling,
   Wisely planned and used with care.

As the stars forth march in order
   Noiseless on their measured way,
So he set his foot firm-planted
   On life's highroad day by day.

Not with gleam of bright romancing,
   Not with far-off dream of glory,
But 'neath stern control of duty
   Working out his human story.

Wise, with clear and far-viewed purpose,
   Steady head, and faithful heart,

To make small things swell to great things,
  This was Arthur's noble art.

In the far East, where Old England's
  Merchant-kings, with proud display,
Taught a false, fierce-blooded people
  To respect a righteous sway ;

Fierce as tigers, false as foxes,
  Who came near them found a school
Where a wakeful soul like Arthur's
  Learned to conquer and to rule.

When beneath French flagellation
  Europe bled at every pore,
Arthur tames a tiger tyrant
  In the Sultan of Mysore.

'Gainst the fierce Mahratta robbers
  Then he marched with measured might,
Wise to foil with nice contrivance,
  Strong with weighty arm to smite.

Cool was he ; but, like a hawk,
    When the moment came he darted,
And was there to crush the foe
    Before they knew that he had started.

While they rage, and while they quarrel
    Who shall plunder most, and where,
With a close-compacted cincture
    Of wise warriors he is there.

There ; but not with tiger vengeance
    O'er the trampled foe to ride,
But in train of armèd Justice,
    With mild Mercy at her side.

Ever prone to peaceful issues,
    But, where seeds of strife were sown,
Firm as flint, and calm as Jove
    High seated on his thunder-throne.

Who shall match his caution, ever
    Slow to strike a doubtful blow ?

Who shall match his courage, never
  Shrinking from a stronger foe?

At Assaye, where bristling warriors
  To his one were counted ten,
Rock and river might not stay
  His weighty push of bayonets then.

He hath triumphed.   Feud and faction,
  Force and fraud, shall rage no more;
Peace shall reign with law firm-handed
  From Nerbudda to Mysore.

He hath based a mighty empire;
  In the East his work is done;
To a sterner task in Europe
  England calls her noblest son.

Shall the pride of Spain be humbled?
  Shall the Frank with iron foot
From the Ebro to the Tagus
  Tramp on law nor fear dispute?

All may fail ; but stout Old England
    Knows to stand the sorest strain :
While she holds the keys of ocean,
    France shall never rule in Spain.

She hath sent her gallant Arthur
    O'er the broad Biscayan flood,
To stay Gaul's rude robber-legions
    From their godless work of blood.

Not with flaunting promise came he
    To avenge the Spaniard's wrong,
But with steeled determination,
    Weak in show, in purpose strong.

As a workman works worked Arthur :
    Not on couch of ease lay he ;
Sleepless oft, or rudely sleeping
    Where a turfy sod might be.

Where a wounded man lay bleeding,
    With quick hand of help he ran ;

Where the doubtful battle wavered,
　　There he stood the foremost man ;

Sharing labour with the meanest,
　　With the boldest risking all,
Standing with his star of honour
　　To maintain his ground or fall.

On the Douro, on the Tagus,
　　Doubt departs when he is nigh ;
Jarring forces chime sweet music
　　'Neath his calm-disposing eye.

But not all were wise like Arthur ;
　　When the sun shone to make hay,
Spanish traitors, London praters,
　　Vexed his soul with sore delay.

Big in boasting, blank in doing,
　　Strong to promise and betray ;
Hollow, windy-hearted, useless
　　To command or to obey.

These would blame him, then, when wisest;
    They might force him to retreat
From the field where lay the vanquished
    Bleeding at the victor's feet.

But he knew to wait: who knows not
    This, shall reap not where he sowed;
Marked by tread of all the heroes,
    Patience is the great highroad.

Showers may come with dark-winged hurry,
    Thunder-clouds pile mass on mass;
But clouds and showers are not for ever;
    Who can wait will see them pass.

On the heights of Torres Vedras,
    With broad breast of bristling barriers,
'Twixt the Tagus and the ocean,
    There he waits their rush of warriors.

Waits and bears, as Ardnamurchan,
    When the western blast is frantic,

Waits and bears, and stands before
  The thunder-rush of the Atlantic;

Waits and bears, and stands, nor fears
  The Gallic Cæsar's banded power;
Massena, Soult, Ney, Suchet, all
  Shall fail when time makes ripe the hour.

Now 'tis come; and, as when hounds
  Rush unkennelled to the chase,
So the fleeing Frenchmen Arthur
  Follows with a thunder-pace.

At Rodrigo, at Rodrigo,
  Lion-hearted, all and each
Leapt with Campbell and with Napier,
  Deft as goats, into the breach.

They have stormed, and they have mounted;
  Like an eagle on a crag,
See, in three-crowned union glorious,
  Flaunting high the British flag.

Where, at Badajos lofty-seated,

Hard-faced walls red flames are spouting,

Kempt and Walker, and the Picton,

Light and buoyant, nothing doubting,

Upleapt to the topmost rampire,

As a rider mounts his steed,

Looking down in pride of conquest,

Where the river floods the mead.

From the heights of Salamanca,

Where they largely learned to bleed,

Eastward, eastward fled the Frenchmen,

Like scared birds with drifting speed !

Arthur to Madrid. 'Mid thunders

Of applausive patriot glee,

Showers of flowers, and smiles of beauty,

Marched the man whose march made free

Spain from galling yoke of bondage ;

Cadiz on the billowy main,

Q

And Seville, with Moorish grandeur,
  Breathes free Spanish breath again.

Onward, northward! Not the Douro's
  Sudden-swelling rapid water,
Not the Ebro, which the Roman
  Oft had stained with Celtic slaughter,

Might give check to hot-spurred Arthur :
  Where he came, their bristling chain
Snapt ; and, in hot drift of terror
  From Vittoria's blood-drenched plain,

Like a cloud they fled ; like locusts
  Swift before the swelling breeze,
Fled the fear-struck myriads Francewards,
  O'er the cloud-capt Pyrenees.

Pampeluna, where proud Pompey
  Stamped his triumph on the rock,
St Sebastian's sea-swept stronghold
  From their bases felt the shock.

On the Bidassoa water,
With well-ordered rank on rank,
Lo! the conquering banner waveth
O'er the proud soil of the Frank!

In the vale where Karl the Kaiser,
With the paladins of France,
Turned his rear-guard on the foe,
And checked the fiery Moor's advance.

As the sandhill owns the spring tide
Swelling strong and stronger on,
Haughty Gaul now finds her master
In the strength of WELLINGTON.

Where he comes the dread tricolor
Pales; the heart of the Garonne
Beats with loyal pulse; the white flag
Flaunts to welcome WELLINGTON.

Onward! blood shall mingle largely
With the blood of the Garonne;

But in vain; the fair Toulouse
  Must vail her top to WELLINGTON.

———————

What remains? look northward; lo!
  God, who reigns in starry hall,
Hath hung forth this flaming scripture,—
  "HE WHO ROSE BY PRIDE SHALL FALL."

From his vauntful, vain believing,
  Down that son of thunder fell;
Fire and Frost conspired to blast him
  With the double scourge of hell.

From the flaming domes of Moscow,
  From Fate's fearful-sounding knell,
From the crumbling of the Kremlin,
  As a falling star he fell.

As Darius from the Scythian
  Wastes, and Danube's swampy swell,

Clothed with shame and crushed with ruin,
   As the proud man falls he fell.

Round him, as a troop of vultures,
   Cossacks hover where he fled ;
Beresina's purpled channel
   Groans beneath her up-heaped dead.

Like a thief that flees from Justice,
   With sharp vengeance in his rear,
Through the storm and through the darkness,
   Lonely, with no helper near.

Vistula and Warta know him
   As they knew him not before ;
Then the master, now the outlaw,
   Pale with rage and red with gore.

All the troops of trampled peoples
   Rise to hound him where he falls ;
Elbe to Rhine and Rhine to Weser
   For a swift redemption calls.

Prussia, from her sore prostration,
　　Stiff old Austria, and the Swede,
Rose, as vengeful Furies rise,
　　To teach the bloody man to bleed.

On the storied plain of Leipzig,
　　Where the brave Gustavus bled,
Ages now shall tell to ages,
　　" Here the French usurper fled."

They have chased him, they have found him,
　　They have bound him, as a man
Binds a bear or chains a tiger,
　　Hateful to the human clan.

They have prisoned him in Elba,
　　In the mid-sea's briny swell,
Iron-hearted rocky Elba,
　　With his own proud heart to dwell.

But not Elba long might hold him ;
　　Like a lion from his den,

Bolting madly 'cross the mid-sea,
  Lo ! he stands in France again !

And a soldier-people rises
  To his call with eyes of wonder,
With the reborn lust of battle,
  Dreams of glory and of plunder.

From the bristling Belgian barrier,
  Like a Jove he thunders down ;
Prussia's Eagle cowers at Ligny,
  From the terror of his frown.

But not England, lion-hearted,
  Flinched till the great work was done ;
Crowned with conquest, braced with purpose,
  Forth she sends her WELLINGTON,

With red scourge to scourge the scourger ;
  Not his eye with terror saw,
Clouds of deathful thunder drifted
  From the woods at Quatre Bras.

Cool as Neptune when his Tritons
　　Bear him o'er the foamy tide ;
Light as Hermes, from the festive
　　Hall at Brussels he did ride

Forth to battle, when the whistling
　　Blasts around him fiercely blew,
Till he stood with calm assurance
　　On high-fated Waterloo.

Stood and faced the Gallic charges,
　　Hoofs of fire, and iron hail,
Firm as granite rock the billows
　　Spurred by the Atlantic gale.

Let them launch their thunder wildly
　　O'er the field and up the steep,
Ever ready, ever steady,
　　English Arthur knows to keep

His chosen ground ; and knows to wait
　　The fateful hour, when, hand in hand

With brave Blücher faithful-hearted,
  He on conquered ground shall stand.

He firm-planted, they wide-scattered,
  Hither, thither, in deray,
With the lawless lust of empire
  Nevermore to vex the day.

And the Power that stirred the slaughter,
  Pride's fell minion, where is he?
To a lone rock they have bound him
  In the far Atlantic sea,

There to chew the cud of self-sown
  Sorrows ; for the gods are just ;
And 'tis written : " WHOSO MADLY
  TEMPTS THE SKY SHALL BITE THE DUST."

www.ingramcontent.com/pod-product-compliance
Lightning Source LLC
Chambersburg PA
CBHW020355030726
47496CB00007B/2149